CLOSER TO SIN

LAUREN BIEL

Library of Congress Cataloging-in-Publication Data

Closer to Sin/Lauren Biel 1st ed.

Printed in the United States of America

Cover Design: Pretty in Ink Creations

Content Editing: Sugar Free Editing

Interior Design: Sugar Free Editing

For more information on this book and the author, visit: www.LaurenBiel.com

Please visit LaurenBiel.com for a full list of content warnings.

This book is dedicated to the readers who still love Enzo despite him being a walking red flag

Chapter One

Enzo

I tried to live the life Gia wanted. Away from the fray. From the lifestyle. But that life called to me. It whispered in my ears and screamed to me from the shadows. I knew she heard it, too. She had to. For someone like her, it would be a goddamn roar. I tried to keep away. Tried. And failed.

I sat across from Jameson, a deck of cards between us and some of his friends. They were talking shop, but the longer I sat there, the more I knew it wasn't about cars at all. What the hell were the O'Rileys into? I was inclined to find out.

"Where's that Silvani girl?" Jameson asked as he shuffled the deck.

"Why do you have such a hard-on for her?" I asked with a bite in my words.

Jameson shrugged. "Who wouldn't?" The other men laughed. "I'd cut my own dick off afterward if I could get one night with her."

"Ain't happening. She's mine."

Jameson flashed his blue eyes at me. "You sure don't act like she's yours."

"You don't know nothing about us." I smirked.

"Girl like that? You better act like it, or she'll hop onto the first dick that does."

I clenched my jaw, causing my cheeks to throb. He knew nothing about our relationship. And even if he did, it wasn't his goddamn business. I rubbed my hand along my revolver, trying to remind myself that Jameson was the only link I had left to my old life.

"Speaking of a *dick*, we need some more muscle to come with us for a . . . thing next week. You feel up to it?" Jameson eyed me.

Yeah, I knew I was a dick. I nodded, throwing my losing hand down on the table. Of course I'd go. What else did I have to do in the middle of fucking nowhere? We were still in hiding after getting rid of Bullseye, and as much as I didn't like to hang around with those Irish pricks, Jameson was the only one besides Gia I could trust right now. They were the only ties to our old life and as much as Gia wanted to be out of it, I still felt the tug toward it.

"And bring that Silvani," he said with a wink.

I stood up, drawing my jacket back and exposing the revolver on my hip. "I'll bring her. But mind your eyes. If I catch them wandering over her for too long, I'll cut them out and feed them to my goddamn dog."

Jameson smirked, throwing up his hands. He thought he was being funny, but he had no idea how far into hell I'd stroll to protect Gia.

THE MOMENT I walked into the house, I was greeted by the big ol' blockhead of mine. He nearly took out my knees as he bounded into me from the kitchen. I ached for Gia before I even got in the car, an uncomfortable throb in my dick at the thought of her. It was all because of Jameson. I fucking loved how much he wanted her, the way he practically drooled all over himself for her.

I pushed Atheist away with my knee and followed the scent of warm thyme and oregano. It smelled like she was cooking up something perfect for dinner, but I was hungry for something else entirely. She turned around as I entered the kitchen, taking a step back when she saw me. I must have looked mad. I wasn't angry with her, no, but I was frustrated as hell.

"What's wrong?" she asked.

"Ain't nothing wrong," I said, gnawing on the inside of my lip. My eyes roved over her. She wasn't even wearing a bra beneath her thin t-shirt, and I could see everything.

When she realized the expression on my face wasn't from anger, she swirled the spoon she was holding, her expression growing playful. "Don't even think about it. I'm cooking."

I stepped closer and rubbed my wrist against her side as I reached behind her and flipped off the burner. She shivered. "You can cook later."

"What has gotten into you?" Gia's eyebrow lifted.

Part of me wanted to tell her how Jameson dripped with excitement for her, but the other half of me wanted that to remain a well-kept secret. What would a girl like Gia do with information like that? She'd use it against me. But I couldn't help myself.

"Jameson wants to fuck you."

"And?" she said in an even tone.

"And nothing. The way he talked about you made me—"

"Jealous?" she asked. She loved to poke me when I was already on edge, and then she wondered why I took it out on her pussy.

I wasn't jealous of someone who looked like he went to church every fucking Sunday. A goddamn choir boy. Gia would break a man like him. Shit, she even gave me a run for *my* money, and I knew what to do with a doll like her. I flashed my eyes at her, dark with hunger. I scooped her up, wrapping her legs around me. She squealed as I tossed the spoon away from her.

"I ain't jealous," I said.

She wrapped her arms around my neck, and I set her on top of the island counter. I'd give her what she wanted this time because I wanted it too much myself. I kissed her. My hands moved down her body, slowing on the soft flesh of her chest beneath the thin fabric that mocked me as it strained against her curves. I grabbed the bottom of the shirt rising up her stomach and pulled until it ripped away from her like wilting leaves. She gasped as my mouth found her nipples, drawing them in and swirling my tongue around the mounds. I took a step back and just looked at her. Her long, dark hair fanned over her shoulders and nearly grazed her perfect tits as she stared up at me. I hated how goddamn perfect she was to me. She could do anything, and I'd forgive her.

She *had* done everything, and I'd forgiven her.

But Gia didn't want a sweet fuck. She didn't want me to fall at her feet and worship her, not that I would. If anyone was falling to their knees in worship, it would be her. Gia wanted to be fucked like she didn't matter and somehow was the only thing that mattered. I would have died for her. I would have killed for her. And I'd fuck her how she wanted to be fucked.

I grabbed her hips with a growl and tugged her off the island. I fisted her hair and wrapped my free hand around her fragile throat, and she bit her lip. She whimpered in my grasp, but it wasn't a sound born of pain; it was from desire. I turned her around, pressing her crotch against the drawers beneath the marble countertop and running my hand downward. With a fistful of her hair, I pushed her chest down until her perfect breasts pressed and rounded against the counter.

"I don't know why I give a shit about who wants to fuck you. That's all you're good for," I snarled in her ear before I yanked down her jeans and worked down my pants. "You just like to be spread open. Used."

I pulled her hips to mine and pushed myself inside her. She cried out, which always made my dick twitch. I loved knowing I hurt her, that I was too big for her. She'd stretch around me and feel so goddamn good in just a few thrusts of my hips, though. Soon she'd be screaming out, begging for her orgasm.

"I like to be used. Use me, Enzo," she whispered through a moan.

I brushed her hair over her shoulder as I drove my hips deeper. "I'll always use you, babygirl, because you're such a *good* fucking whore."

My final words bit, and a single tear left the crease of her eyelids and fell down her cheek, a perfect sphere of the pain she felt in that moment. It weakened my resolve, and I found myself wanting to comfort her. But I knew her. It was what she wanted. She'd get fucking pissed if I tried to comfort her. Wherever all this brought her in her fucked-up little head, she liked to stay there for a while, conquering whatever demons she needed to confront. I didn't know why she liked to go there, to the darkest recess in her mind, where all the shit she buried went to rot. Nah. I'd never understand it. I didn't dare wander into The Outlands, where bones would lie all around me and phantoms would haunt me. That girl was something else.

"Tell me more," she whispered through clenched teeth.

I shed my hesitation. "Don't even look at me," I hissed as I fisted more of her hair and forced her to look at the tile backsplash. "You get my cock, and that's it. But that's all I am to you. Right, Giovanna? Just the cock you need to make you forget about how worthless you feel."

She nodded, letting a moan fall from her lips. "I don't deserve your cock, but I need it, Enzo," she whimpered. She pushed back on me, sending me deeper into her. I groaned as my hips rocked her ass, slapping against her skin.

"You know I won't let you come, right?" I asked. When I used her like that, I didn't let her come. I didn't reward her for wanting to be degraded. Maybe one day she'd stop needing to be fucked like I hated her.

She nodded once more, biting her lip as I drove my hips further and faster. She spasmed around me, tightening against me.

"But I'm going to come, and I don't care if you want it or don't. I'm going to fill your *incredible* pussy."

She huffed at my compliment, but I couldn't say anything negative about what was between her legs. She was perfect. She stretched around me like I was meant to be inside her. Like she was made for me.

"You want my come, don't you?"

"Please," she whispered.

I stopped thrusting and stayed buried inside her as I came. I'd have given Gia anything, the world if she wanted it, if we weren't in such a mess. If I hadn't needed to strip myself of my power to keep her safe, I'd have given her back the lifestyle she ran from but so clearly belonged in.

Chapter Two

Gia

Ringing bells and electronic blips filled the air as people pulled the levers on the slot machines. There was an ebb and flow of excitement around us as some won and others lost. Anger and happiness converging in one space. Women in short skirts strolled through the room, carrying trays of water and alcohol. Jameson called one over, smacking her on the ass before taking a rum and coke off her tray. He slipped her some cash, and she giggled before dropping the bills down the front of her shirt. The O'Rileys owned the casino, and it was situated outside of town, so we were safe there. Even though I didn't particularly *like* them, we didn't really have issues with the Irish. Just everyone else.

The dealer squinted at me, waiting for my move. A ten and two. Useless. I tapped my fingers on the table, and the dealer threw another card down. Enzo wasn't much of a gambler, but he wanted to watch me play.

"Bust," the dealer said as a queen of hearts hit the table. He dragged my losing chips to the center and stacked them.

I also wasn't much of a gambler, clearly.

The dealer looked at me to see if I wanted to buy in again.

"I'm no good at this." I shifted on Enzo's lap and looked at him.

He pulled the cigarette from his mouth and blew the smoke into my face. It swirled and circled around my head with a warm, rich aroma that made me crave one as well. He smirked and put the cigarette between my lips, where I held it. Jameson couldn't keep his eyes off me, and we all noticed. He'd brush his blond hair back every time he tried to fight the desire to look at me. Enzo shifted me once more on his lap so that I was facing Jameson.

Enzo leaned into my ear. "Play, and don't drop that cigarette from your lips," he whispered, his warm breath making me shiver because I knew what he meant.

Enzo smirked at Jameson before he spread my legs on his lap. I inhaled a sharp breath, which sent way too much smoke into my lungs. I fought the urge to cough as his hand rode up my thigh beneath the high-top blackjack table. I tried to focus on the two cards resting in front of me on the felt as the dealer stared at me. Enzo rubbed me through my panties.

Seven . . . seven and two . . . I tapped the table, and the dealer tossed out another card. King of clubs. Nineteen. No bust.

With tight lips, Jameson chose to stand. The dealer flipped his second card, matching Jameson's eighteen but losing to me by one. My hand trembled as I raked the chips into my pile. I dug my fingers into the plastic of one as the smoke blew from my mouth harder than it should have. It was damn near impossible to keep control as Enzo played with me under the table.

He's out of his goddamn—

I couldn't moan or I'd drop the cigarette. The fragile ash grew longer at the tip, and one spasm of my body would knock it loose and drop it onto my lap. Enzo was hard as fuck beneath me.

Jameson kept glancing between my legs, his hard cock visible through his jeans. The dealer dealt out another hand. I gripped the wooden side of the table for dear life as Enzo's finger made circles around my clit. The dealer knew what was happening, but he pretended he didn't. My legs trembled. It took so much work to keep the moans in my throat, because the moment they rose from my vocal cords, they'd explode from my lips. My abdomen sucked in, trying to give my body anything else to focus on besides the growing pleasure between my legs. I kept my eyes on the dealer's twirled mustache or the uneven stack of chips in front of me. Enzo quickened his touch, and I tightened my lips on the cigarette, trying to keep it balanced between them. The dealer dealt my cards and just as I was about to come, I snatched the cigarette from my mouth.

"Blackjack!" I screamed as a queen and an ace landed in front of me. The word was so laced with my orgasm that it was impossible to hide. Heat flushed my cheeks and when I looked back at Enzo, he was smiling. *Fuck you.*

Enzo dropped his hand from between my legs and grabbed my other thigh, pulling them together possessively. I wiped ash from the table. Jameson's fair skin was mottled red, either from anger or being turned on, maybe both.

"I'll meet you at your room in the morning, Jameson. Balance the books then," Enzo said as he pushed me off his lap. He grabbed me by the waist and tugged me toward the casino's exit.

He was still hard as we got to the elevators. The bell rang above us and the doors spread open, welcoming us inside. Enzo hit the button for the seventeenth floor. I held the "door open" button as I fumbled with Enzo's pants. He wiped his chin and smirked, shaking his head. He looked up at the camera.

"No, Gia," he commanded.

I let go of the button long enough to undo his pants and slip the zipper down. I eased him out of his boxers and hit the "door open" button once more. I needed more time. I was good with my mouth, but I wasn't thirty-seconds good.

His eyes glanced at the cameras above him again. "You know Jameson's family owns this casino, right?"

"I know," I said with a shrug. I ran my fingers along the buttons, hitting every floor before seventeen, and allowed the door to close as I dropped to my knees. I took Enzo into my mouth. As the floor turned to two, he tensed. The doors would open at each floor, potentially putting us on display. I took him to the back of my throat.

"Goddamn it, Gia," he groaned as his fingers gripped the metal handles behind him. The floor turned to three, then four. Every *ding* made my heart race, waiting for the lurch of the elevator and the doors to open. He fisted my hair and guided me faster and deeper on his cock. I gagged, but fought back another one.

Ding. Ding.

The elevator kept ascending, my nerves growing raw with every floor that passed. "You couldn't wait five minutes to get your mouth on me, could you?" he groaned.

I shook my head. It seemed fair. And yet even then, it was much more private than what he'd done to me out there. The elevator climbed further, closer and closer to our floor. I knew Enzo was riding his ascent too as he thrust his hips against my mouth, making me take him as deep as I could. Tears rolled from the corners of my eyes, smearing my makeup.

"I'm going to come," he groaned. Just as the elevator made a final *ding* before the doors spread open, his warm come hit the back of my throat. He held the button to keep the doors open as I licked up his twitching dick. He grabbed my chin in a rough grasp. "Good girl."

Chapter Three

Enzo

I grabbed a bottle from the minibar in our room. Gia was fast asleep, but I couldn't sleep. Even working with the O'Rileys caused an itch that grew until it felt unscratchable. I drew a cigarette from my pocket and lit it, slipping out onto the patio to smoke. As I closed the door, it slid along the track with a squeal.

The bustle of the casino created an extra beat in my heart. I missed my old goddamn life. I looked through the patio door's dingy glass and stared at Gia's bundled-up body in bed. I missed my old life, sure, but I couldn't imagine any life without Gia. She destroyed everything in her path like a wrecking ball, and yet I couldn't stay mad at her for ruining everything I'd worked toward. When I brought her to my home, I never expected *that* to become what this turned into. I thought there'd be some good hate sex, we'd get paid, and she'd go on her merry little way as a goddamn Silvani. She'd do her thing, and I'd remember how she felt on my dick for the rest of my life. Instead, she shook everything up and broke me. I wasn't some weak fucker looking for *love*. I didn't *need* anything she had to offer besides what was between her legs. Neither of us *wanted* what happened between us. She forced us into a new life where neither of us had a damn choice. I was terrified to love, but I was more afraid of losing her.

I never used to be scared of shit.

I drew in a deep breath of smoke, letting the nicotine weasel into my bloodstream. I wanted to take on the damn world with her by my side, but it couldn't happen, even if I somehow got back to the city. She was an untouchable. Well, not so much *untouchable* as much as it was incredibly fucking dumb to touch her. We could never be whatever we thought we could be. I couldn't go home and run my household with her. A goddamn Silvani. What a conflict of interest. I'd never be able to make the right decisions when it came to her family with the swell of my dick clouding my judgment.

I closed the door as I came back into the hotel room. I slipped off my dress shirt, leaving my ribbed t-shirt in place. I glanced back at Gia before leaving the room. The sounds of gambling drew me like a moth to a fiery flame. I knew that shit was illegal. No family in this lifestyle conducted legal businesses. Not fully, at least. That meant the underbelly of that place was seedy as shit, and I was curious to find out what it was filled with.

The big metal door slammed behind me as I took the staircase down to the basement. Sweat dripped down my temples as I reached the last stairwell. My gun weighed my hip down on my right side. I walked down a long, dark hallway. The old fluorescent lights flickered on and off. I was definitely in the underbelly. It was disgustingly silent, without an ounce of music or casino noise. My steps echoed off the walls. I tried doors on my way down the hall, but all were locked. My eyes caught a glimpse of a toolbox by the wall. I dug around for anything I could use to pick the lock of the handle that showed the dark grease of use on the metal. My hands found a small screwdriver, and I kneeled and envisioned the internal mechanism as I put it into the lock. I worked it until it popped open for me. Sweat dripped down my cheeks, and I wiped it away. Keeping my hand on my revolver, I opened the door and stepped into the dark room. Motion sensors flashed and filled the space with light.

I walked into an office. There were business ledgers everywhere. I looked through them. It was textbook laundering. The paper trail looked clean enough to pass an inspection, but being in the business, I could easily see the way they moved the money around. I flipped a few more pages until my eyes snagged on a name that made my mouth go dry. I turned back to the page.

Bianchi. As in Bullseye fucking Bianchi.

My lips tightened. Had I brought Bullseye's car to someone who worked with his goddamn family? I hated when another family held something over me, especially something as big as Bullseye's murder.

The trip to the basement had satisfied my curiosity and then some. I learned more than I bargained for.

I locked the door behind me as I left the office and made my way back up the stairs to the main floor. I ran into Jameson just as I passed the gaming floor. Sweat was still collecting on my temples.

"Enzo! I didn't expect to see your face out of that room," he said with a tight smile.

"I had to go for a walk," I said in a calm, even tone.

"You can't just walk around our casino with that." He gestured toward the revolver on my hip.

I rolled my eyes, untucking it from the holster, slipping it into the waistband of my pants, and concealing it with my shirt. It hid it at least somewhat.

"Come have a drink with us," he said. It wasn't a question.

I followed Jameson down the hall to the presidential suite and into the room. A half-naked stripper gyrated to the thumping bass from the overhead speakers. The men in the room passed drugs around. About twice the party I expected from the Irish.

I took a seat in one of the overstuffed chairs, and Jameson rustled through the minibar. He pulled out clear bottles of vodka and tossed me two of them. He picked whiskey. One of the girls eyed me and sauntered over on heels that made her long legs even longer. She leaned down, her bare breasts beside my face. Glittering gold eyeshadow encased her dark eyes.

"Hey," she said with a smile. She sat on my lap with a flirty look in her eyes.

I twisted the cap off the vodka and downed one of them. "Barking up the wrong tree," I said.

She tightened her lips, taking my words as a challenge. Her hand slipped down my chest and toward my lap.

I grabbed her wrist, stopping her descent. "I said no." She was a beautiful girl, no doubt, and her tits in front of my face were tempting, but I'd rather return to my room and take out my frustration on Gia's body than slip my dick into this one. "It ain't you," I said as I touched her cheek. It shined with heavy makeup. "I got a girl."

"So do most of the men," she whined as she gestured around the room.

"Mine would castrate me and feed my balls back to me if I touched another woman." I laughed. It was true.

"She wouldn't know . . ."

I rolled my eyes. Gia would know. I couldn't lie to her, and even if I could, she was like a damn bloodhound when it came to deceit. She'd just know. The girl tried to slip down on her knees anyway. "Get up," I said, stopping her hand from riding up my thigh. This girl was fucking relentless. "Fuck this," I said with clenched teeth just as her hand grabbed at my dick. I wasn't playing with some broad who couldn't take no for an answer. I stood up, knocking her back on her ass. She huffed at me, and the man in the corner —her bodyguard—raised his pistol at me. I reached back and grasped mine. "Teach your girl some manners," I hissed at him, pushing his gun out of my face.

Jameson rushed between us, holding up his hands to placate the angry guard. "Hey, hey! We're all friends here, so no need to get your hackles up." He patted the guard's beefy shoulder and motioned for him to resume his post. He turned to me. "I don't blame you for that. Jess can be a pushy bitch when she smells new blood . . . and money. But maybe you'd do better to spend some time with that Silvani instead of down here with us. Don't want to draw too much attention, if you know what I mean."

Yeah. I knew what he meant, and now I wondered if I'd already fucked myself by bringing Bullseye's car to his doorstep. I'd handed Jameson the ammo and he could pull the trigger whenever he felt froggy enough.

I went back to my room, frustrated and angry. More angry than frustrated by that point. At least the girls at my club knew when to stop. I put my gun on the bedside table before unbuckling and undoing my slacks. I slipped into a pair of sweatpants and crawled into bed with Gia. She wrapped her arm around my waist, burrowing into my chest.

Nah, ain't no girl worth it, I thought as I brushed Gia's thick hair away from her cheek. I rubbed the front of my pants, trying to soothe the throb of my dick. I wasn't going to wake her up just to fuck her. She knew my body, though, and despite thinking she was asleep, her hand dipped beneath the waistband of my pants. "Gia," I groaned. "I'm not in the mood." I was in the mood, but I was too angry to think straight, to fuck her right. I gripped her wrist and drew her hand away from me. My dick twitched in protest. I knew the type of person I was. I'd fuck her so goddamn selfishly if I tried right now. I'd rip her apart.

She huffed and turned over, and I wrapped my arm around her and pulled her closer. She grinded her ass into me, but I grabbed her hip with a rough grasp, halting her movement.

"Trust me, Gia, you do *not* want to do that right now," I growled in her ear. She did, but I wouldn't let her. I had far too much to think about. Things could go south for us with the O'Rileys, and I needed to figure out how to get ahead of it.

Chapter Four

Gia

I smoothed my dress down my thighs. The mirror fogged as I wiped away a smidge of red lipstick that had ventured beneath my lower lip. It felt good to get dressed up again. I missed the life more than I thought I would. I walked into the living room and found Enzo. He was dressed up as well, wearing slick black slacks and that purple dress shirt I loved.

"Goddamn it, Gia," he groaned as he pulled me onto his lap.

"Don't we have to go meet Jameson?" I asked.

With a sigh, he checked his watch. "Yeah. Fuck, let's go."

We drove winding roads on our way to meet Jameson and his crew. "Isn't the Irish mafia sweet? Jameson sweet?"

Enzo scoffed. "Jameson isn't sweet, nor are the Irish. Don't let their jovial demeanors fool you. They can be vicious bastards."

"What are we even doing for them?" I grasped my pistol

on my thigh. When Enzo told me to bring it, I knew he wasn't sure what would happen either.

"Who the hell knows."

We pulled up to the bottom of a long driveway at an address Jameson had jotted down in sloppy and rushed chicken scratch. Enzo looked out the window and crumpled the paper in his hand. When he got out of the car, he met with Jameson and his group. My mouth dropped open at the amount of guns and close combat weapons, like brass knuckles and a baseball bat. *What the hell are we doing?* I got out of the car to wolf whistles. Jameson hushed up his men and flashed me a smile. I dropped my gaze.

"Wait, why did we bring a broad with us?" one of the men behind him quipped.

"Who do you think he's going to let in?" Jameson gestured to the house on the hill.

Enzo stiffened. "I brought Gia to watch our backs while we handle shit, not be the face."

Jameson swung his arm around Enzo, squeezing him. "You know what I did for you? Right?"

Enzo's lips twisted into a frown, and I knew he wasn't comfortable entering unknown territory with me at the front of the pack. I pulled him back toward the car. "I'm fine. I've done worse." I shrugged.

He pulled me into him, kissing me so damn hard I thought I might become one with him. But I knew why he'd done it. He wanted Jameson to know I was owned, and that was confirmed when he glanced at the Irishman as he released me from his grasp.

My heels spread rocks as I made my way up the gravel walkway, stones crunching beneath each step. I put my hand on the gold knocker, rubbing my fingers along it before announcing my arrival. The men hid on either side of me, in the shadows created by the home's sharp angles. I waited. I looked at my phone before tucking it back into my bra. Just when I turned to ask the men what I was supposed to do, I heard footsteps on the other side of the door. Locks twisted and the door slid open. A middle-aged man answered.

"Can I help you?" He narrowed his eyes at me before letting them drop down and hover on my chest.

"Can I use your phone? My car broke down at the bottom of the hill."

The man stared at me for a moment, peering down the hill toward the road before stepping aside and waving me in. I glanced sideways at Enzo, who was being held back by Jameson. I expected them to jump in sooner, and my heartbeat quickened in my ears. The man looked behind me before closing the door and locking it. I swallowed hard and clumsily leaned my back against the door to steady myself so I could turn the lock as I bent down to slip off my shoes.

"My phone's back here," the man said as he motioned me down a long, dark hallway.

There was practically a runway of red flags leading to the man in the silk bathrobe, but I didn't show him how nervous he made me. I followed him with sure steps as I felt for the reassurance on my thigh.

When we got to the kitchen, he unplugged his phone from the charger to hand it to me, but ripped it away at the last moment. "Who sent you?"

"Excuse me?"

"Broad like you didn't get herself stranded in the middle of *my* nowhere. No one comes this way unless they have reason to." He stepped into me and put one hand on my pistol and the other between my legs. "Could you be a debt repayment?" The man's graying mustache covered most of his upper lip. I leaned away from him as his fingers dug into the flesh of my thigh. "If you tell me who sent you, I'll know who owes me what. Then I'll decide how much you're worth."

Come on, Enzo.

Just as the man went to take my pistol from my thigh, the sounds of guns cocking echoed around me. The men came in, guns drawn. Enzo was at the front of the pack, his revolver aimed and his finger on the trigger when he saw the man's hands on me.

"Get your fucking hands off her," Enzo hissed.

"The O'Riley brothers," the man said.

"In the flesh," Jameson quipped. "We got business to discuss."

"Hanging with the Italians?" the man asked with a laugh.

"Long time friends, is all," Jameson said.

Enzo rolled his eyes. He motioned me over to him and I went to his side, where I felt safe.

"We ain't paying," Jameson said, "and we're gonna need you to forget the little debt we owe you."

"You owe me two hundred grand, Jameson. I am not just 'forgetting' that. Your gambling problem is a you problem." The man turned his attention to me. "But maybe . . . an arrangement—"

"Not happening. I should shoot you in the dick just for thinking about it," Enzo snapped. His cheeks throbbed through a clenched jaw.

"Oh good, my men have arrived." The man clapped his hands together as another echo of metal on metal came from behind us. Guns were drawn on us, and our guns were aimed at the man.

The men behind us were huge. Enzo was the closest one to being as muscled as them. I swallowed hard, recognizing the eerie familiarity between this and being in front of the Russians. The twitch in Enzo's expression made me certain it was familiar for him as well.

Before we knew what was happening, the men had grabbed hold of Enzo, and the man in the robe snatched me from his side.

"If you do this, I will fucking kill you. And everyone you ever loved," Enzo said in an even tone, but I knew it was taking everything in him to not explode. An explosion would only get one or both of us killed. His wide, desperate eyes broke my heart, so I forced myself to look anywhere else. At the artistic vase in the hallway across from me. At Jameson's stupid fucking face. At the metallic row of guns aimed our way.

The man bent me over the kitchen table. I bit my lower lip so hard I drew blood. I couldn't even hear the words being yelled from Enzo's mouth over the thunder of my heartbeat in my ears. My dress bunched up and my cheeks flushed with heat. This was not going to happen again. I would not be used as a goddamn bargaining chip.

"Wait!" I called out.

The man stopped. I pawed his hands away and turned to face him. I leaned into him and kissed him, his mustache tickling my nose. I had a plan, but I couldn't look at Enzo as I followed through with it, because I couldn't bear the look of betrayal on his face.

I hopped up and sat on the table and spread my legs. Jameson stared between them as I ran my hand up my thigh. The man in the robe was on me, kissing my neck as he rubbed over the fabric of my panties. I let a fake moan leave my lips. When he was preoccupied with pulling out his dick, unashamed of what he planned to do to me, I reached into my bra and tucked my pocket knife into my palm, putting it down on the table and covering it with my hand. The quick hit of the button on its side flipped it open, cutting me. It took everything in me not to react to the pain. Just as he pulled my panties aside, I grabbed the handle of the knife and stabbed it into his neck. I didn't hesitate as I drove the knife deeper. He didn't react at first, too stunned as the blood spread around the blade. I threw my gaze to Enzo and we both drew our pistols. Before they realized what was happening, I shot at the men behind our group. Enzo took down two and I took down the other. Their bodies hit the ground with a nauseating thud. The man between my legs stumbled back, clutching his neck as blood spilled from his mouth.

Enzo slammed Jameson against the wall. "You fucking piece of shit. Selfish goddamn micks, all of you. All you guys do is drink, fight, and gamble. Poorly." Enzo shot his gaze back at me. "Did he?"

I shook my head.

"You're lucky he didn't touch her, or I'd kill you myself."

I was covered in blood. Mine and whoever that piece of shit still bleeding out on the floor was. I tugged my knife from his neck, and the blood flowed freely, finally giving death the chance to welcome him.

"Your problem is done," Enzo snapped at Jameson as we walked past him. "Now fuck off."

"We'll call it even," Jameson said as we exited the home.

I glanced over my shoulder in time to catch the devilish smirk on Jameson's smug face before Enzo pulled me through the doorway. We hurried down the driveway and climbed into Enzo's car.

"That fucking prick!" Enzo shouted as he slammed his door. "He would have let that happen to you. He was willing to put *my* fucking girl in a shit situation because of a debt he can't pay. Fuck!" He rammed his palm against the steering wheel before starting the car and leaving a spray of gravel and dust in his wake.

Before I could respond, my phone buzzed in my bra. I pulled it out and glanced at the screen. A notification for a text message from an unknown number popped up at the top of the phone, and I clicked on it. My stomach lurched.

It was an image of Enzo chugging a drink with a bitch on his lap and her tits in his face. Another message came in, this time displaying an image of the same girl on her knees in front of him. I glared at Enzo. Anger rose from the very depths of my being. I heard Enzo talking, but I couldn't hear the words. All I could hear was some bitch's moans as she choked on Enzo's dick. I gnawed at my cheeks.

Attempted murder? Attempted rape? Homicide? Those things didn't matter to me, but infidelity was a different story. Everything that had grown between Enzo and I just fucking died. Everything we had been through was reduced to nothing but wilted petals beneath a bare rose stem. How could he?

"Pull over," I said.

"What?"

"I said pull over!"

He brought the car to a stop on the side of the road not even a half mile from the scene of the crime we'd just committed, but I didn't care. This needed to be handled immediately. I got out of the car and he met me near the trunk.

"What's the problem?" he asked.

How dare he fucking ask me that question. He knew what he did. He knew *who he did.* I tossed the phone at him.

His eyes widened as he viewed the pictures. "Are you fucking kidding me? You know nothing happened."

My cheeks flushed with heat, my chest rising harder with anger. I drew my pistol and aimed it at Enzo. It was a knee-jerk reaction, and it wasn't smart, but it was what I fucking wanted to do. My hand was sure and steady, my finger against the trigger guard. I saw nothing but red. I was the embodiment of a Silvani at that moment.

Enzo aimed his revolver back at me. "Put your goddamn gun down, Gia."

"You can't tell me shit when you do something like *this*." I gestured toward the phone still in his hand. "Fucking Vigliones."

Enzo stepped into me, grabbing my wrist and bending it away from me as he disarmed me. He slipped my gun into his pocket. "I'm back to not trusting you," he said through clenched teeth.

"I'm not the untrustworthy one," I snapped. I was so angry that it made the blood in my veins feel hot.

Enzo grabbed my arm and dragged me toward the car. He tossed the phone onto the passenger seat. I shook my head, not wanting to go with him. I'd take my chances on the desolate road in the middle of nowhere. I dug my heels into the grass and mud. Enzo turned back to me and squeezed my arm.

"We have to go. We can deal with this later. Away from the scene of a goddamn murder. Well, multiple murders."

"I don't want to get in the car with you."

A breath of desperation blew from his mouth. He pulled his gun out and put it up to my head. "Get in the goddamn car, or I swear to god—"

"You'll what?" I narrowed my eyes.

"Don't make me do something I won't want to live

with." His lips tightened, and the fierceness in his eyes made me back down. There was a psychotic darkness to them.

"Fine," I said, pushing the barrel of his gun away from me.

Nothing is fine.

Chapter Five

Enzo

I couldn't believe how tonight went. We were used to being the ones shaking down the money, not the ones being shaken. That was not a side I wanted to be on. I was the predator, not the fucking prey. Everything that happened tonight was over rightfully owed money, and Gia wasn't a fucking payment for their debt. Those Irishmen had no goddamn dignity.

Gia wouldn't look at me, but I felt the heat radiating off her from the seat beside me. She burned me with her anger. She had bandaged her hand with tape, blood still staining her skin.

"Gia," I began.

She scoffed. "Don't bother."

I was fucking pissed. Between her anger and mine, I was worried the car would burst into flames. I knew Jameson had sent those pictures because Jameson was a fucking prick. He knew I stopped that girl. But he also knew an opportunity when he saw one. An opportunity that would thoroughly fuck the relationship I had with Gia. Trust had already been a problem. She betrayed me once, and now she thought I'd betrayed her.

I would never.

"Throw your little tantrum now because when we get to the house, you're going to fucking listen to me talk. Understood?"

She didn't respond. Just brooded.

When we got back to the house, she got out of the car before I could stop her. She unlocked the door and let Atheist out, who charged to greet me. I waited outside on the porch for him to take a piss, and I dreaded how I would explain things to Gia. I didn't do what she thought I did, but the truth sounded like a lie.

I dragged Atheist in by the collar and slammed the door so hard that the decorations on the wall rattled. I went into the guest bedroom and found Gia rummaging through her bag.

"What are you doing?" I asked, crossing my arms over my chest.

"Leaving."

"The fuck you are."

She stopped shoving shit into her bag and faced me. "You don't get to tell me what I can and can't do."

There were so many layers to what we needed to talk about, but I wasn't sure which one to pick through first—the bitch, the murder, or the attempted rape. The pictures of that woman made Gia forget all about the murder. She pushed that shit way to the back of the line. I'd discuss the pictures first.

"You know I wouldn't fuck around on you."

"I thought I did." Her lips tightened. "Pictures don't lie."

My lip twitched. "They don't tell the fucking truth, either."

"You're honestly trying to deny that you let her suck you off?"

Jesus H. Christ. I couldn't figure out how to give a rebuttal. *Fucking Jameson.*

"I kicked her off my lap because she wasn't taking no for an answer, and I left."

Tears glassed Gia's eyes. There was nothing in her that believed me, and it was killing me. Her eyes widened in realization. "That's why you didn't sleep with me that night," she whispered.

Fucking A. What a night to have a goddamn conscience and not fuck her. I didn't fuck with the girl but damned if it didn't sound like I did.

I stepped into her, snaked my hand behind her neck, and pulled her into me. "If you think I'd ever fuck some other girl when I've got you, you don't think enough of me. You're the only thing I want to sink into, the only person I have ever fucking loved. I didn't fuck you that night because I found some shit at the casino that had me worked up, and I didn't want to hurt you."

"I never gave a shit if you hurt me, Enzo. Have I ever? Have I ever told you to stop? That you were too much?"

"I mean . . ."

"Have I ever said it and meant it?"

Her words were ice cold, but she was right. Even when she told me no, she never actually meant the word.

I knew what I needed to do to show her she was mine. I kissed her, and she pushed against my chest.

"Fuck you," she hissed.

Our bodies were rigid with anger and stress. I fisted her

hair and turned her around, bending her over the bed. She fought against me.

"I don't want this, Enzo!"

"I do," I growled in her ear.

I risked pushing her into hating me more instead of forcing her to want me, but it was a risk I was willing to take. I lifted the skirt of her dress, a tremble in my touch for a moment as I saw the blood splatter on her inner thigh and remembered the part of tonight she refused to remember. I pulled her panties aside and worked my pants open.

"Don't, please," she pleaded. Her cheeks were red with either anger, fear, or arousal. Who the fuck knew what else she felt?

I knew Gia enough.

I spit on my hand and rubbed my cock before pushing it inside her. She was warm and wet for me. She cried out, letting her chest fall forward onto the mattress.

"You're mine, and you need to be reminded of that." I thrust every syllable into her. She fought against me, but the twitch of her pussy as I fucked her told me all I needed to know. "Goddamn it, Gia." I drove my hips forward, pushing her deeper into the mattress.

"You're hurting me," she said through panting breaths.

I knew I was. She had reached the edge of her limits, and I pushed well past them, much like the night Atheist had been shot and I let my frustration boil over. She trembled beneath me, gripping the quilt with her blood-stained hand. I selfishly fucked her, just like I tried to avoid doing. I didn't care if I made her feel good, I just wanted to pour my frustration into her. I needed her to know she was mine.

Guilt brewed in my belly. I couldn't tell if she wanted me to keep going or to stop. The wise thing would have been to stop. But I couldn't. She felt too damn good and I *needed* to come. I'd make it up to her. I leaned over her, drawing her ear toward me by her hair.

"I fucking love you, Giovanna, and I swear on my mother, I didn't touch that girl." I grinded my hips against her ass, giving her a break from the relentless thrusts. She melted into the mattress. "I need you to trust me. We ain't nothing without it."

Her pussy clenched around me and I drove her hips forward with mine as she came on my cock, screaming out in pain and pleasure. Ain't no way I would stop her from coming, not after tonight. Not after everything that happened. I welcomed the squeeze of her pussy as she tightened around me and came. Her spasms drew my orgasm from the surface it bubbled beneath, and I filled her as she rode out the final waves of her pleasure. I pulled out of her, the head of my cock shining with my come. I pulled her to her feet and kissed her. She didn't fight me or push me away. Instead, her eyes flashed up at me, soft and round with satiation. My come dripped in a pearly line down her thigh, and I bit my lip. I interrupted its path, catching it on my fingers as I slid them up her thigh and pushed them inside her, making sure she had every drop of me within her. I kissed her once more. She was mine, and she had to know it. I needed her to know that I would do anything for her . . . except allow her to come every time her body begged me for more.

Chapter Six

Gia

I woke up alone in the guest room. Enzo had let me stay there alone last night. I promised him I wouldn't go anywhere if he just gave me some goddamn space.

It was hard to imagine him doing something that would hurt me like that, but it was even harder to erase the images of that girl from my mind. Her hand on his thigh. Him chugging a drink to forget about me. Her round ass as she was on her knees in front of him. It taunted me in my head. Even though shit hit the fan and splattered against everyone in that home last night, I could only focus on that bitch. The image became a movie of how I thought things happened. It replayed over and over again, and the more I saw, the angrier I got. Just as I began to believe Enzo's story, the replays boiled my blood until it scalded my insides.

Enzo came into the room and stared at me. He scanned me with his eyes, trying to read me.

Don't bother. I'm fucking illegible.

"Can we talk yet?" he asked. He was shirtless, and gray

sweatpants hugged his hips. He'd worn that on purpose. Without an answer, he walked in and pushed me over so he could sit on the bed. He grabbed my hand, unwrapping the peeling tape, and looked at the cut on my palm. "We gonna talk about what happened?"

"Which part?" I snapped, still riding my anger over the scene in my mind.

"All of it," he said as he pulled some antibiotic ointment and a bandage from his pocket. He started to dress the tear in my skin. "We committed quite the murder. Well . . . murders."

"Who was that guy?"

"Mr. Arnold. An independently wealthy man with no real ties to any of us. He liked to invest. He shouldn't have invested in the Irish, though. No-good pricks. But he was a very influential man, and his death is going to make waves." Enzo swallowed hard. "But you did what you had to do."

"Do you really think so?" I dropped my gaze.

"It was either your knife or my bullet. No matter what, he was going to be dead for trying to fuck you."

I found it interesting he talked about who wanted to fuck who when I saw what I saw. He had some nerve to care about who was going to fuck me when it sure as hell wasn't him who was fucking me that night he played around with some whore.

"You care so much about who was trying to have sex with me, but not about you cheating on me?"

"Gia—" he said in a stern tone, but I cut him off.

"If you didn't fuck with that girl, Enzo, what were you doing in the hotel room with her?"

"It's not an *if*, Gia. I didn't." He scolded me with his expression. "But anyway, I broke into their office. The O'Rileys are laundering, which is no real surprise. But . . ." He shook his head. "What had me worked up was that they were or are still somehow involved with the Bianchi family."

My jaw dropped open. *Bullseye? The one rotting in the lake? Oh god.* That meant Jameson definitely had too much on us, something very big that he could dangle over our heads for as long as we lived. And if he told anyone? We'd be fucked. After what happened last night, I was certain he'd tell someone. Anyone.

"What are we going to do about Jameson?" I asked after a long pause.

"Well, I could buy his silence with what he's been drooling over . . . or we can kill him." Enzo shrugged. "Or do nothing and hope he keeps our secret for us. I'll kill him before I let him fuck you, so it's either that or nothing."

"Fuck him? It'd be fair, right?" The words came out harsher than I intended. In Silvani fashion, I took a stab when I saw an opportunity to do so. He made me feel stupid, like I was crazy and overreacting, but I *saw* the picture. Nothing in his expression in the image looked like the rejection he claimed it was. I wasn't stupid, and I refused to be led on. Being alone would have been better than having this constant movie playing in my mind, wondering if it was fiction or not. I didn't trust anyone easily, and I realized why. Not a single man I'd been with had earned it and kept it.

Enzo's lips tightened, his cheeks flushing red with anger. "Is that what you want? To whore around with that Irish prick?"

"I just think it's my goddamn decision. Doing nothing isn't an option. Killing him is fucking unwise. If he wants me, let him have me. Such is this life, remember?" I didn't want to sleep with that piece of shit, but I was so fucking mad at Enzo—or the situation. I couldn't tell any longer. I just said what I could to hurt him. "Besides, you didn't give a damn about me in those pictures."

Enzo rose to his feet and leaned over me with fire in his eyes. I had pushed him past the point of anger and into some world where I was suddenly the enemy again. "If only you knew how untrue that was. Fucking Silvani. Goddamn hypocrite." He spit the words at me.

I kept my chin up, unwilling to cow to him. Yes, I was a goddamn Silvani.

ENZO COULDN'T EVEN LOOK at me as we walked to the car. I got in and crossed my arms over my chest. He wrapped his hands around the steering wheel and tightened them. I recognized the old hatred that simmered between us when I first got to their home. The toxic sexual chemistry had dissipated, replaced by anger and mistrust. But I wouldn't apologize, and he sure as shit wouldn't, either. We were much too stubborn, which was a trait bred into us.

It was a stalemate.

We were stupid for ever thinking what we had could work, that we could sleep with the enemy and somehow be a happy goddamn family. We *were* enemies, and we'd always end up that way, one way or another.

We were finished, and that was the way it had to be.

Bile churned in my stomach at the prospect of sleeping with Jameson. I'd handled worse, but I thought Enzo would be the last person I'd have to give myself to. No one could or would fuck me like he did. When Enzo degraded me, it made him uneasy because of how much he disagreed with the things I wanted him to say. That made me come that much harder. But I felt obligated to do what I was planning to do. Jameson knew something that would get me and Enzo killed, regardless of whether we were together or apart. I hadn't pulled the trigger, but I was still a part of it. I was doing it for myself. For my family. And a little for Enzo, too. A *little*.

We drove over familiar roads on our way back to the casino. I offered to go myself but even when he loathed the blood coursing through my veins, he refused to let me go alone. I told myself it would be quick and easy. Jameson had always been hard for me, so I didn't expect him to last more than a few minutes. It would be transactional.

We walked into the hotel, assaulted by the sounds of machines ringing and murmurs of people all around us. Lights flashed, tantalizing my senses. The ambience almost made me feel high.

I followed Enzo to the presidential suite at the end of the hall, and he knocked, folding his arms across his chest as he avoided my gaze. Jameson answered the door with a tight smile.

"You're the last person I expected to see," Jameson said to Enzo before his gaze met mine.

"And you're the last one I want to see," Enzo snapped. He pushed his way inside.

"What do you want?"

"Why didn't you tell me you guys dealt with the Bianchis?" Enzo's chest puffed out as his posture stiffened.

Jameson's cheeks flushed. "It's our business."

"You know what that could mean for me, right?" Enzo asked.

"Yeah." Jameson shrugged.

"Gia here wants to give you a reason to be quiet about

it," Enzo said in an even tone as he went to the fridge and grabbed two small bottles of vodka. He chugged them.

Jameson's eyes jumped to mine, his head cocking in curiosity. "Which means?"

I bit my lip, trying to explain to him what I was offering without speaking. I didn't think I could say the words I needed to say without them getting stuck in my throat. A smile crept over Jameson's face. I expected more hesitation out of him as he stepped into me and kissed me. He had no suspicion in his kiss as his hands roved downward, grabbing my ass.

"If you'll keep your mouth shut about Bianchi, you can fuck me," I said. The words were woven tight with anger, but he didn't care. All he could think about was being inside my pussy. "Do we have a deal? I need you to tell me," I said as I leaned away from his prying tongue.

"I'd tell you anything you wanna hear if it means I can fuck you." Jameson was a mess, so deep in his frustration and excitement he didn't even seem present.

I put my hand up to his chest and pushed him away. His posture stiffened and he resisted my attempts to stop him. "That's not what I asked."

"I won't tell a soul, Silvani," he growled as he closed the distance between us once more. His lips trailed down my neck.

I shot a side glance at Enzo, half hoping he'd stop whatever was about to happen. He just leaned back against the counter and crossed his arms. How was he okay with it? Why wasn't I? I'd bartered with my body more times than I could count. I loved to be fucked like I was only something to be used because that's all I'd ever been. My body had always gotten me things I wanted and gotten me out of things I didn't. Why did I suddenly feel like my body didn't belong to me any longer? Wasn't mine to give away?

When Enzo turned his gaze from mine, releasing me from his possession, my cheeks flushed with anger.

"In front of him?" Jameson pulled away to ask me.

"I'm not his anymore," I said.

A sadistic grin crossed Jameson's face. "Goddamn, Gia, I've dreamed of this," he growled as he spun me around and pulled me into him. His hard cock pressed against my ass, and his hungry hands rubbed down my sides as he bent me over the couch. I looked at Enzo, his cheeks pulsing with anger, but he wouldn't face me.

I moaned, trying to incite some reaction from him, some way to force his gaze on mine. Jameson tugged down my pants, fisted my hair, and forced me to look forward. I stared at a yacht in a framed picture in front of me. His buckle came undone. His zipper and a nauseating wave of guilt followed. Jameson's touch ignited the nerves in my skin until they became unbearably warm. It was as if his fingers were hot enough to brand me. Just as I was about to stop it from happening, there was a sound of a silenced gunshot. My heart leaped into my throat, and I thought I was going to throw it up. The air thickened with the metallic scent of murder.

Jameson fell to the ground behind me, not even a breath of sound leaving his mouth. Blood splattered against the wall, and I tugged up my pants and looked at Enzo. He had Jameson's pistol. A silencer was threaded on the barrel. His eyes were an aggressive shade of blue.

"What the fuck, Enzo!" I screamed. That was *not* part of the plan. That was *really* fucking dumb, actually.

"I couldn't let him fuck you, and it was too late to do

nothing," he said with ice on his tongue. He threw Jameson's phone at me. "I'll meet you in the car."

I looked down at a bloody and very dead Jameson. Dark crimson saturated his golden hair and spread in a thick puddle around his head. My stomach twisted less at his dead body than it had at the idea of fucking his live one, though. I looked down at the phone Enzo threw at me and saw the picture he had pulled up. It was him standing up and the girl on her ass, anger on her face. Her bodyguard had a gun drawn on Enzo.

My heart broke. He'd been telling the truth all along.
Fuck.

I almost let Jameson have sex with me. What the hell was I doing? Did I not have an ounce of self-worth in my goddamn body?

Jameson's phone vibrated in my hand. I looked down at the text.

One mill for the pussycat.

I drew a quick breath. *Oh god, no. Please, no.* Everyone called my father pussycat, like the damn cartoon.

Chapter Seven

Enzo

F*uck Gia.* I was disgusted by what she'd been willing to do, how she'd have let that son of a bitch fuck her if I hadn't stopped things. I scoffed. I hated her right then, but I still couldn't watch her get fucked, couldn't imagine another man feeling her perfect pussy around his dick. That was the only thing that was perfect about her. Her smart-ass mouth and Silvani attitude made her imperfect as fuck. I thought I could look past the blood coursing through her veins, but clearly neither of us could.

I fucked up, though. She was right, even if I hated it. We were on camera at his family's hotel after murdering Jameson, all because I couldn't stomach her handling a . . . business transaction.

What a goddamn mess.

The passenger door flew open so hard I thought it would break off the goddamn car. Gia sat down, her eyes wide with fear, and I ain't ever seen fear on Gia's face like that, not even when I put a gun to her head or someone threatened to take her pussy. There was usually a cold, stoic expression on her face that reminded me she was a Silvani. But not this time.

"What's the—"

"There's a hit out on my father." Her words came out in a flurry.

"Wait, slow down, Gia. Explain."

"On Jameson's phone. A text came through that said one million for pussycat. That's my father, Enzo."

I rubbed the back of my neck. *Goddamn it.* Talk about being between a rock and a hard place. We were between a murder and a hit. If we stayed here, we faced repercussions from the O'Rileys. If we went back to the city, we faced my brothers. We'd face every damn family that considered my back turned on them. But I knew Gia. She'd go whether I went with her or refused. She'd go home to her father herself. What she didn't realize was that there were hits on her, too, before we left. How could one target protect another? They both had goddamn bullseyes all over them. And on top of all that, like a plump cherry, was the fact that she didn't trust me. Didn't believe me. And fuck her if she thought I was going to risk myself for someone who didn't even trust me.

"So what?" I said with a bite to the words as I slammed the car into reverse to get the hell outta Dodge.

She blinked hard beside me, and her mouth dropped open as if she expected me to leap at her words, jump like a dog to run into a war I wanted no part of.

Gia crossed her arms over her chest. "Take me home." She squinted her eyes. "Back to my father's."

"Whatever you want."

DRIVING into the city made my palms sweat. Atheist panted between us as I drove the familiar gridlocked streets to bring Gia home. Her home. She was so preoccupied with the text she saw, she didn't care to mention the pictures that proved I didn't do what she thought I did. She didn't even look me in the eye as she gathered her bag, petted my damn dog one last time, and slammed the car door. It took everything in me not to follow her, but I refused to chase her. I couldn't. It was better this way.

My head still cocked as I watched her walk away, at the sway of her full hips.

Fucking Gia.

I drove toward my family's house, unsure what I would walk into. My brothers weren't all that forgiving—I'd been the weak one to forgive Gia much too easily after she infiltrated our family—but they didn't know her like I did. No one did. I knew the person beneath her façade, the one who needed to let herself be weak in order to love.

I pulled up to the long driveway, took the familiar turn, and drove until I found myself at the front of the mansion. As I pulled into the garage, the dam in my mind broke and flooded me with memories of Gia. With a long breath, I got out of the car and headed to the front door. The moment I stepped inside, guns were drawn on me, and holding them were people I grew up with, the people who raised me, even. A look of discontent washed across their faces, and I deserved it. They knew I'd run off with a Silvani, but beyond that, I didn't know what they knew. They had to know that Bullseye was missing. Shit, they may have known that Jameson was dead.

I didn't raise my hands in defeat or beg for forgiveness. I wasn't going to beg for shit. I was the oldest. The business was mine.

I met Marco's narrowed eyes. As the second oldest, he'd have taken up the role, but he was interim at best. Marco would be a good leader one day, just not today. He looked nothing like our father, and his quiet-but-deadly demeanor was the opposite of the brazen nature of our departed patriarch. He was the silent, brooding type. He'd breathe new life into the business one day.

"What you doing back here?" Marco asked, the silver barrel of his pistol in my goddamn face.

"Taking back what's mine," I said with a shrug of my shoulders. The empire *was* mine, regardless of the pussy I fucked or what lapse in allegiance I let happen. Enzo Viglione was next in line for the proverbial throne.

"Over my dead body, Judas," Marco hissed.

"That can be arranged." I put my hand on the butt of my revolver.

I liked Marco more than I liked Sammy, but I wouldn't let him consider what was lurking in his mind. Sammy, the baby of the family, reminded me way too much of Silvio. It wasn't his fault, of course, but I saw it in the way he leaned against the wall or puffed on a cigar. He was Silvio's boy.

"Get your fucking guns out of my face. If you wanna fight over it, I'll take ya, Marky." I smirked at him, rolling up my sleeves. Marco waved his hand, and the men lowered their rifles.

"I'll take you," Marco said as he tugged off his t-shirt.

I stripped off my dress shirt, leaving my ribbed t-shirt on. I had more muscle and height than Marco. He was foolish to get into anything hand-to-hand with me, but if that's what it took to get him to stand the fuck down . . .

Sweat crept onto my temples as we walked toward the library. Marco's jaw clenched, his bare skin beading with sweat along his back. I pushed open the library doors. It would be easier to clean the blood from the slick floors there.

"Alright," Marco said as he squared off against me. He raised his hands to block his face in a defensive position.

I stepped back and drew my hands up, my fists firm in my line of vision. I let him make the first move, swinging at me with guarded force. I struck back, unguarded and full-strength. My fist made contact with his face, sliding along his cheek. Blood splattered from his mouth as he bit his lip from the force. He took a step back, crimson dripping down his chest, and charged at me, throwing his body weight into me. His blood stained my shirt as I braced against him. Marco threw hooks at my ribcage, and I felt the crunch of a rib or two. My breaths faltered for a moment as I harvested energy from the pain and jabbed punches at his head. Unearthly noises rose from the depths of my stomach as I punched until he finally backed away, faltering in place. He looked as if he might tip over if I touched him. He shook his head to recover. I couldn't react before he was on me again, leaping at me. I landed an uppercut to his jaw with a scream of frustration boiling over from so much more than that moment. He fell backward and I leaped on him, pinning him at his hips and drawing my arm back again. His eyes went wide, and my hand trembled in place. I couldn't bring myself to punch the bloody man beneath me. His eye was swollen and bruised already. Blood leached from his nose and ran down his chin and neck.

"Are you fucking done?" I snarled.

"Fuck you." He spat the words out, along with more blood.

"Are you really in the position to be so goddamn hostile?"

"You're fucking the bitch who killed our father." He writhed beneath me.

Goddamn it. Another great time to gain a conscience. "Gia didn't kill him."

He wiped blood from his mouth. "Then it was her pops!"

"I fucking killed Silvio." I dropped my gaze before glancing toward Sammy. His fists were clenched at his sides. Marco stopped writhing beneath me and stared up at me with wide eyes. Well, the one was wide. I panted above him. "I did it."

Marco tried to throw me off by lifting his hip, but it was futile. "Wh-why?"

"You won't believe me if I told ya, but he *deserved* it."

"Ain't nothing he could have done to deserve being killed by his own goddamn flesh and blood," Sammy said behind me. Their reactions verified what I always knew, that they were never touched. Fucked around with. Made into a goddamn show.

"I'm glad you say that. That means you didn't go through what I did. Be grateful." I climbed off him.

In a way, it was comforting. But it also meant they'd never understand the depths of pain and mistrust Silvio created. The degradation stole my dignity, ate away at my worth. To fuck a whore while your own fucking father jerks off to you . . . *Fuck you.* I couldn't even think about the rest without conjuring up more memories, forcing me to live with them.

"Silvio was a sick fuck. That's all I'm willing to tell you." My eyes narrowed as I offered my hand to help him to his feet. With hesitation, he took it. "Leave Gia the fuck out of it. She and I are done."

Chapter Eight

Gia

How the hell was I going to explain what I knew? I needed to tell my father about the hit. I needed to make sure his men kicked up their protection. But I somehow had to explain how I found out about it, where I was when I learned of it, and who I had been with.

The enemy.

I stood in my kitchen, my mind swirling as my fingers tapped on the glass of a vodka bottle. I wanted to down as much of the bitter liquor as I could. Maybe it would restart my heart, which felt like it had no beats left. My chest was silent and still. It felt vacant. Being alone in my head in the big kitchen made me realize just how fucked everything was.

I should have trusted Enzo. I should have known. Enzo loved me. I loved him. With everything against us, we were somehow making it work.

Ro walked into the kitchen and jumped when he

spotted me. He nearly dropped the glass in his hand. "What the hell are you doing here?" he asked with suspicion all over his expression. Suspicion I deserved.

"I'm back," I said.

"From where?" He cocked his eyebrow.

"I needed time to clear my head."

Ro squinted at me. "Time with *him*?"

Fuck. I knew that would be the first thing they thought. And they were right. I ran off with the man whose family I was supposed to infiltrate. He was supposed to be a faceless casualty, a pawn in the family game. Enzo wasn't shit to me back then. He was a speed bump on our way to the top. But then I got to know him. He suddenly had a face. Instead of a speed bump, he was a whole person standing between us and our goal. When he protected me from his uncle, handed me the gun to take my vengeance, I got feelings. When he preyed on my fantasies and desires, bringing them to life for me, those feelings grew wings. As I fell for him, he made me fall in love with the business once more. I wanted to be a part of it again.

"You don't have anything to say?" he said as he set the cup down in front of me.

What was there to say? I was a traitor. I chose Enzo over my own flesh and blood.

The worst part? I'd do it again.

"There's a hit out on our father," I said as my fingers squeezed around the vodka bottle.

Ro cocked his head. "A hit? How—"

I shook my head. "Don't ask me how I know. It's better if you don't know."

"Are you sure?"

"Positive. Is anyone else called pussycat?"

"Fuck," Ro said as he wiped a hand through his hair and exhaled. "You know there's a hit out on you, too, right?"

My jaw went slack. "Wh-what?"

"People think you killed Silvio."

My eyes widened. "What?" *Oh fuck.* "I didn't kill Silvio!"

"*We* know that, but try to tell that to his brothers. You being here just brings more heat on us."

"So what? You want me gone?"

Ro shook his head. "You can't stay here."

I swallowed hard. Where the hell would I go? I purposely isolated myself the last few years, trying to pull away from the business. I wanted to make a clean break. Or try to.

I racked my brain, trying to think of someone I hadn't already fucked or fucked over. I had *one* place I could go, and it was with someone I never thought I'd have to ask a favor from.

My eyes locked on Ro's, pleading without words but knowing he was right. I couldn't protect my father if I was drawing heat of my own. "Fine, but promise me one thing . . ."

"What?"

"Protect him, but don't tell him I told you," I said with a defeated drop in my shoulders.

"I won't," he said as he drew me in for a hug. I held my arms out at his affection. It felt as if he was saying goodbye. He wasn't allowed to say that to me. Not yet.

MY CAR SMELLED like me with a hint of lingering cigarette smoke. I was glad to be back in my own vehicle. My hands on my own wheel. What I didn't like was where I was heading—to the home of an old friend who'd been out of the game long enough to have become obsolete. The only person who could provide a sanctuary for me.

I drove through busy city streets until I parked in front of a high-rise building. Apartment windows lined its walls. I leaned back and let my eyes crawl up until I spotted a soft light where his apartment was. I got out of the car and walked to the stoop and hit the button on the call box. A loud buzzing broke the silence.

"Hello?" came a drowsy voice from behind the speaker.

"I'm here to visit Rosario Esposito. Apartment 402."

"Is he expecting you?"

"No," I said as calmly as I could.

"Please hold while I call him for approval."

I leaned against the flaking concrete, tugging my jacket closer to my body. The light flickered above my head as I waited for the man to return. He never came back to the call box, but the sound of the heavy door lock disengaging told me he'd accepted my strange, unsolicited visit.

My heels clicked on the shiny black-and-white tiled floor in the lobby. The security guard waved me off as I walked toward the elevator. The moment I hit the button, the doors spread, and soft music welcomed me inside. The ascent to the fourth floor felt like an eternity in the older elevator, and I felt every lurch on the way up. The bell rang and the doors spread open. I took a moment to ground myself and tried to remember which way his apartment was. I went left, heading down the long hall until I reached the door labeled 402.

I took a long breath before knocking. I listened for the

footfalls behind the door. He'd had to have known I was coming. I finally heard the footsteps before the chain unlocked. The door swung open.

"Hey, Rio," I said with a smile.

He cocked his eyebrow at me as he leaned against the door frame, his full lips tight as he kept his eyes narrowed on mine. His hair was sloppy and brushed back. "Why oh why do I have a Silvani on my doorstep again? What kind of trouble are you in?" he asked as he kept his body firmly between me and his home.

I twirled hair around my finger as I stared at his sharp jaw. "Well . . . people think I killed someone." I flashed my eyes up at him, giving a hint of a flirt, trying to get him to at least let me inside.

"Did you?" He crossed his arms over his chest.

"Not this time."

Rosario groaned and stepped aside, allowing me to enter. The place was beautiful. My eyes widened at the big windows. Artistic furniture that probably came with the place littered the big living room. I sat on the angular couch that was a shade of yellow I surprisingly didn't hate. It somehow fit in the room of grays and blacks.

"So you gonna tell me why the hell you're here?" Rosario asked. His words were harsh, which was fair. I used the hell out of him before he left the business, and there I was, using him again. "Last I heard, you were abducted."

My jaw went slack and I rolled my eyes. "I was not abducted." My lips tightened. "I was with Enzo Viglione."

Rio made a face like he thought I had to be joking. A soft chuckle ensured that he did. When my expression didn't change, his laughter stopped. "Wait, really?"

"Yeah."

"Well, I'm disgusted I thought you were still so damn

sexy." He curled his lip. "I wouldn't touch a Viglione if I was in the throes of death and one of them was the only cure." He shook his head. "Nah."

I chuckled. Did anyone actually *like* the Vigliones? I didn't even like the Vigliones. I just liked Enzo. His shit family was just part of the package deal. Rio disappeared down a hallway and came back into the room, racking his pistol.

I raised my eyebrows. "You don't need that. We're done."

He scoffed. "You clearly don't know Enzo. He's never done. If you're what he wants, he'll have you."

"I don't think—"

He stepped closer, put his tall, dark presence in front of me, and leaned over to raise my chin. "You may be a Silvani, but you're the most addictive woman I've ever slept with." His jaw set. "Trust me when I say he isn't going to forget about you."

His words burned through me. I slept with Rosario to get to his family. He was a notch in my belt I'd never forget. He was also one of only a few men I slept with who were still living and breathing. Probably because he'd gotten out of the game.

I was the reason his father's empire had fallen. They were bottom feeders now. We thought we were meeting their family the day Silvio was killed. Rosario paved the way for one of his brothers to take over their father's legacy. Or lack thereof. The family was crumbling enough that Rosario was allowed to slip through the cracks and live a life in a boring upscale apartment in the heart of the city.

Like a ghost from his past, I came and haunted him.

"Don't get ideas," I said.

"Nah, I wouldn't fuck with Enzo's girl. I'm not about to

get myself killed, not even for that pussy of yours." His cheeks flushed with heat. "Would it be worth it?" His eyes rushed to the ceiling in thought. "Almost." Rio sat beside me and put the gun on the coffee table in front of us. He dropped his head into his propped-up hand and turned on the TV. "You can stay for a couple nights. And I don't wanna know nothing about what you did."

Chapter Nine

Enzo

I was trying to keep my mind on too many things. Trying to figure out business. Keeping an eye on the bounty for Gia's father and making sure my brothers were actually standing down regarding Gia. I was the boss now, a position I'd been working toward since I knew what the word meant. Nothing would go on that I didn't know about. I wouldn't reign with a blinding fist like Silvio, though. He lost sight of what we needed to do to stay in power. His focus had shifted too much. To what? I wasn't even sure. The stacks of paperwork in the office made me think he didn't know, either.

Even when I felt like I had everything I ever wanted, ever dreamed of, I was missing something I considered just as mine as the goddamn business. I shook my head. That couldn't happen. We had to be done.

I stiffened at a knock on the door and swiveled around in the chair that Silvio's ghost probably haunted. My fingers grazed the big wooden desk. The door swung open and

Marco approached with determined steps, his footfalls echoing in the empty library. His eye was still bruised and swollen.

"Did you know there's a hit on Gia's father?" Marco asked as he slammed his fists down on the desk. "Is that why you came back? Because of her goddamn father?"

I sucked my teeth before rising to my feet. I leaned over the desk, drawing closer to Marco's face. "I knew there was a hit, yes, but it ain't your business why I'm back."

"It's my damn business if she's the real reason you're here and not because of the family."

My cheeks flamed red. "I killed an O'Riley, that's why I'm back."

Marco cocked his head. "One of the Irish?" He narrowed his eyes. "Why am I certain *she* had something to do with that, too? Why can't you see that death follows that girl? She's nothing but trouble."

"You know who you sound like? Ma." I scoffed. "Don't talk to me like you're the older one, little brother."

"Is killing her the only way to get your mind right?"

I closed my eyes and took a deep breath. "If you or anyone else lays a goddamn finger on Gia, I'll kill you."

"Ah, there it is." Marco smirked as if he'd caught me in the trap he'd set. "I won't let you ruin our family with an allegiance to a goddamn Silvani. I won't allow it."

I knew he wouldn't allow it. I knew going back into the city that Gia was more my enemy now than ever. Before I killed the fucker, I left Marco to go cool off using the one thing I knew would help me relax.

THE DRIVE WAS EERILY QUIET. Gia wasn't there to mess with my radio or distract me. It left me stuck in my own head, which was a real shitty place to be trapped in. I didn't *want* to jump right back into my old ways, but the old me knew the only way to get me out of my head. I got out of the car and rolled up my sleeves as I walked into the club. The smell of salt and perfume hit me the moment I opened the door and the music thumped in my chest. Women danced on the three main poles in the center of the room, and my favorite dancer was one of them. We called her Socks because she always wore knee-high tube socks. Somehow, she made it look sexy as fuck. She smiled as she slipped her body down the pole until she was on her knees. She crawled toward the end of the stage, beckoning me with her eyes. I walked over and lifted her chin with a firm grasp. She licked her lips.

Even if I didn't want it to be, part of me was being tugged back by Gia. If I was the normal Enzo I'd always been, I'd have taken Socks off the stage, paid her for her time, and broken all my club rules. But I wasn't normal anymore.

I wanted to be, though. I'd try to be. I was going to force myself to be Enzo fucking Viglione.

I grabbed her hand and dragged her off the stage and toward the back rooms, passing signs that warned me to keep my hands off the dancers. ABSOLUTELY NO SEX was underlined in black marker. I pushed Socks into the closet-sized space and kissed her. I wouldn't put my lips on any other dancer, but Socks was special. I turned her around and pressed my body against hers, pinning her against the wall. I growled as her ass poked out and rubbed against the front of my slacks. My hands trailed down her bare, sweat-sticky sides before landing on her bony hips. She felt nothing like Gia, which was maybe a good thing.

She started to ease down her panties, but I grabbed her wrist and stopped her. I couldn't bring myself to fuck her, even with her warm body against mine. I turned her around to face me and kissed her again. I bit her lower lip as her hand worked my zipper down.

"Get on your fucking knees," I said as I pushed her to the ground.

Her hand continued to work off my pants, and she pulled my cock from the confines of my boxers. I dropped my head back, my eyes closed. I tried to focus on the feeling of her fingers on me as she wrapped her hand around me. I fisted her dark hair, but a nagging feeling in my gut made my lip curl. It wasn't her, she didn't do nothing wrong, but I couldn't go through with it. Just as she went to take me into her mouth, I grasped her hair and stopped her. She whimpered. I tugged her off her knees, and disappointment washed across her face.

"It ain't you, Socks," I said with a stroke of her cheek.

I zipped up my pants and grabbed my wallet, thumbing through bills and handing them to her. Her eyes lit up at the money, and I smacked her ass as she left me in the booth. I looked at my reflection in the mirror with a frustrated glare. I refused to admit that I stopped her because of Gia. Nah. But what other reason was there to push a beautiful girl away from your throbbing dick?

Goddamn it.

I let myself cool off before I headed toward the back of the club. I pushed through the metal door and watched the eyes turn toward me. Some were glad to see me, but others pinned me with accusatory stares. The seat where Bullseye always sat was vacant, and I felt a tinge of guilt.

"Enzo," Kenny said as he rose to his feet. His jaw was slack, surprised to see me.

"Where's Bullseye?" I asked, even though I knew.

"MIA. Gone for a couple weeks now."

I pulled a chair out and sat down. "Shit."

A lanky man stood and held his hand toward me. "Vinny Giordano, no relation to the watchmakers. I've taken over Bullseye's runs. I'm not a shot like him, but I can hold my own."

A laugh tickled my throat and made me run my tongue along my teeth to keep it inside. Dude looked like a salesman, not someone who could make the threats needed to secure payments. My eyebrow rose.

"I've worked with Bullseye for years. You'd have heard by now if I wasn't capable."

He was right, I would have, but I couldn't get past the shady tax-accountant look he had going for him. "Yeah," I said. If he could work, then work. I didn't care. As long as I got paid.

Kenny's eyes kept jumping to me, as if he had something to say. I hoped he would keep his stupid mouth shut and not ask about Gia. I didn't need the questions, and none of them would believe the answers.

"Your brother was doing a fine job, Enzo," came a voice from beside me. The man stood, slipped his hat from his head, and placed it on the table. Antonio Lucci. He was the big lug who always hung around, silent and brooding, like my brother. No wonder they got along so well. He was damn good at intimidation and encouraging people to pay, even when they had nothing to give. His size didn't scare me, though, nor did his inflammatory words.

I stood, squaring off to him. "Marco isn't next in line. I am."

Antonio stared at me, his eyes narrowing. "Your father dies and you vanish for weeks, then you come back, throwing your weight around. Who the hell do you think you are?"

I knew I'd get flak for disappearing. I never intended to return, so I didn't exactly prepare anyone for my absence. I deserved the mistrust. I was fucking surrounded by it these days.

Tony puffed his chest at me. My fingers itched to draw my pistol on him, but I didn't have a room to back me any longer. The murmurs of my desertion would get every gun turned on me instead. I had to stay cool, but staying calm and collected wasn't exactly my M.O.

"I know you guys don't trust me right now, but I had reasons to leave for a while. Things I can't even begin to explain. But I'm back, and my head is where it needs to be. I'm asking for a chance to prove I can run things like my pops . . ." I swallowed. "Better than Silvio." I sat down.

"Your head isn't what I'm worried about, Enzo," Tony said. "That damn Silvani girl of yours has you by the balls."

"She and I are done."

"Yeah, she's shacked up with Rosario now," Vinny said, trying to help my case.

My gaze snapped to him, my eyes narrowing. *Play it cool.* "We're done," I repeated.

Tony waved me off and dropped back into his chair. I heard the whispered *fuck you* that rolled over the card table and fell into my lap. My skin flamed hot, but I stayed cool.

I waited until the men filed out to go back to work. Liquor bottles and empty glasses were strewn about the card table. I got up and started to pick them up. Glasses clinked together between my fingers as I set them on the bar top. Vinny opened the back door to leave.

"Vinny," I called.

He stopped mid-step, hesitating before turning toward me.

"Rosario Esposito?" My question drifted across the empty room. He shot me a quick nod before turning around and hurrying out of the building.

Fucking Espositos. They were a weak family, falling apart and holding on to the lifestyle by a thread. They weren't even being snatched by the feds one by one like most of us. Nah, they were just disemboweling themselves. Rosario was their oldest son, the next in line, but he'd rejected the role and wanted nothing to do with the business. Which was fine, but why the fuck was *my* business hanging around *him?*

I threw a glass at the wall, and shards spread across the floor as they fell. I didn't even bother to stay cool. I was so on fire. I was burning.

A part of me, somewhere deep down in my gut, said she would be safer moving on. And staying away from her damn house. The larger part of me, that boiling-hot part, completely rejected the idea of her being around another man, especially one who could be fucking good for her.

No. She was mine.

Even when she wasn't with me, she was mine.

Chapter Ten

Gia

My car idled on the hill. I had to see my father to know he was still okay. I finally spotted him, surrounded by security and my brother. He was protected. He was safe. I waited until they were out of sight before I drove off, knowing I couldn't let them see me.

I drove back to Rio's apartment on autopilot as the standstill traffic tested the very last bit of my patience. When I got to his building, he buzzed me up. The security guard waved at me as I walked by. I took the elevator to the fourth floor and wandered down the hall toward Rio's room. The hair on the back of my neck prickled, and I spun on my heels to look behind me. The hallway was empty. Silent. It felt as if someone had been watching me, but it was only my mind playing tricks on me.

I glanced behind me again before knocking on the door. Rio let me in and I hurried into the apartment. I didn't dare tell him about my irrational fear of being followed. He'd throw me out on the spot. If someone was after my father, they could be after me too, which meant I'd put Rosario at risk.

"Did you see a ghost?" Rio asked as he touched my cheek. My skin felt hot. I worked to calm my breathing. I wasn't scared, but I felt uncomfortable.

"No, just a little on edge is all." I stepped away from his touch.

"Are you going to tell me what's going on with you?" he asked as he blocked my path.

"Hard no."

He folded his arms over his chest. "Then I can't be your safe harbor, and you should go find somewhere else to lay low."

I scoffed. I didn't have anywhere else to go. "If you must know, there's a hit out on my father."

Rio chuckled. "There's been a hit on all our fathers at one point or another."

"Some shit has happened that makes it more than just a threat, and it mostly revolves around the Vigliones."

Rio closed the gap between us. His dark eyes bore through me, unearthing the guilt I felt for using him in the past. "A woman like you isn't the type to run and hide. What's got you so scared? I don't think I've ever seen you frightened." His hand reached out and caressed my cheek, but the tender touch nauseated me. Rio was a kind lover. Sweet. A man who would make a wife really happy one day. When I asked him to degrade me, to give me some pain, he looked at me like I had somehow offended him. It had nothing to do with *him*. It kept my mind off everything but the weight above or behind me. It's how I'd forget every- thing and everyone that hurt me. I was in control by giving up mine. Every time he fucked me, it was slow and deep. Sensual. Like he loved me. That wasn't what love felt like for me. Weighed down with thoughts that kept me from ever getting to the edge, I never came when I was with him.

"Rio . . ." I met his eyes again. "Don't."

I knew what he wanted. The tented fabric of his jeans made it clear. I thought about it, believe me, I thought about it, as a way to buy time to let me stay with him a little longer. He ignored me, leaning into me and drawing me in for a kiss. I couldn't do it. I pulled away from him, away from lips I'd kissed so many times before.

"He'll know." I didn't know how he'd know, but he would, and he'd kill Rio for touching me. Another side of me piped up, reminding me that I wasn't Enzo's anymore. He made it clear that we were through. But I knew he still cared about me, and that alone made him dangerous.

Rio didn't deserve the trouble it would cause if I let myself slip away from Enzo and into Rio's tempting arms. I wasn't ready to comfort myself with the first dick that presented itself. Rio was a free man, and I refused to force him back into the life by letting him inside me. The moment he fucked me, he'd be part of it, whether he wanted to be or not. I shrugged out of his touch, calming my rising chest.

✦

Enzo

I PRESSED my gun against the maintenance man's head as I dragged him toward the fourth-floor room.

"I have children," the man pleaded, his lanky body struggling to keep up with my determined steps.

"I ain't gonna hurt ya," I hissed. My eyes tracked the numbers on every metal door. When we got in front of 402,

I put my finger up to my mouth, shushing him. "Unlock the door, and if you tell a soul you saw me, I'll come for you. Do you understand?" I shook him by the collar of his tan button-up shirt. He nodded furiously as his fingers trembled when he tried to find the right key to open the lock. "Give it to me." I jerked his head down when I pulled the keys from his retractable lanyard. I tried a few before I found the master. When I released them, they jerked back and hit the man in the face, cutting his chin. He ran off, looking back at me with every furious click of the elevator's call button.

I opened the door and saw Gia's face close to Rosario's mouth. In a single motion, he drew his pistol on me, as if he'd been waiting for me. I pulled out my revolver and cocked the hammer.

I didn't particularly like Gia right then, but what I saw still made me see red. She was like a toy I wasn't allowed to play with, but I also didn't want anyone else to play with her, either. Was I being selfish? Abso-fucking-lutely.

"Speak of the devil," Rio said with a curl of his lip.

"Fuck you. What are you doing here, Gia?"

She crossed her arms over her chest and stared at me. "I needed a safe place to lay low."

"This ain't a safe place. People know you're here. Someone I didn't even know knew you were here. How do you think I found out?"

Rosario looked at Gia and then back at me. His face paled.

"No one gives a shit about you. Relax." I shut the door behind me. "Did you fuck?"

Rio laughed. "Not in quite a few—"

"I'm not asking you, I'm asking *her*." My eyes remained on hers. I'd know if she lied to me. Her lower lip trembled when she lied. I stepped toward her, but Rosario put his body between us. "I ain't gonna hurt her." I shouldered past him. "Did you fuck him?"

Her eyes narrowed. "No, you piece of shit." Her lower lip was steady. "Now I'd like you to leave."

Rosario interrupted. "I'd like you both to leave, actually."

I smirked as Gia's gaze jumped from me to him. "Oh, fuck you both," she groaned.

"Where else you gonna go?" I asked her as we drove toward my house.

"I don't fucking care where I go, but I'm not going home with you. Bring me to a hotel or something."

I rolled my eyes. "There's eyes all over this city. You ain't going to a damn hotel."

"This is feeling eerily similar to when you abducted me."

It felt that way for me too. Grumpy, petulant Gia in the backseat of my car once more. I looked in the rearview mirror and stared at her the same way I had that night. Everything was different, though. When she first stayed with me, I'd only had her one time before that, a distant memory that gnawed little holes through me every time I heard her family name. Now I'd really had her, and the air in the car had shifted. Resentment and mistrust hung like smog around us. She broke my trust, and I broke hers—even though I didn't. But I was still willing to protect her. I just had to figure out how to explain it to my goddamn brothers.

The silence remained between us as we pulled into the underground garage, and a heavier silence engulfed us as I turned off the car. Water dripped from a pipe that created a rust-colored path away from the wall. I walked to her side and pulled open the door. "Come on, Gia. Stop being so damn ungrateful." She knew what I had risked by bringing her back to my home.

She leaned back with a huff, increasing her antics and testing my patience. I got sick of playing around. Sick of the cold, damp air in the goddamn garage. I grabbed her arm and pulled her out of the car. Her lips were tight as I righted her and pushed her toward the door.

We walked inside and took a right down the familiar long hallway with the big mahogany door at the end. The moment she realized where she was going, she stormed off herself, leaving me behind as she slammed the big wooden door.

I rubbed my knuckle along the wall, trying to figure out what to tell my brothers. How could I explain why Gia was here and why I'd brought her to the home of those who considered her the biggest target of all?

I had taped the damn bullseye to her back and sent her down range.

Chapter Eleven

Gia

The bed was how we left it the night Lorenzo tried to rape me. The blanket was still strewn. It still smelled like that vile man for a moment, and I couldn't tell if I had merely imagined it. I didn't want to be here again. Not like this.

It felt too similar.

It felt all wrong.

I shouldn't have felt like a damn prisoner. Not again.

I grabbed the hem of my shirt and went to lift it off. My eyes caught the black camera in the corner of the room, having forgotten about its presence. I tugged my shirt back down. My eyes narrowed, though, as I kept them locked on the little round piece of plastic.

I was fucking pissed. Angry about being back in that room. In his home. With him. I was going to do just fine without him. Eventually. How dare he come into Rio's apartment like a brute and threaten him. He did nothing wrong.

I looked back up at the camera. I knew what would make him feel some of the anger I was feeling. A bit petty, but . . .

I took off my shirt, then my bra, and I bit my lip as I looked up at the camera. I slipped out of sight and locked the door. I grabbed the wicker chair tucked beneath the desk in the corner of the room and planted it in the middle of the floor in the direct line of the camera. I sat down, lifting my skirt as I did. After playing on my phone for a moment, I spread my tan thighs, exposing deep-red panties. I drew my legs back together and spread them every so often. When I heard no footsteps, no reaction, I went further. I pulled my panties to the side, exposing everything I knew he wanted. My hand ran between the valley of my breasts, cupping them before I let it wander lower.

Lower.

Until I dipped my fingers into the warm excitement between my thighs. I ran my finger through the slick wetness, up and down, slow and sensual, as I kept my eyes trained on my phone screen. I looked at the camera as I slipped my fingers inside me. When there were still no sounds and no footsteps, I dragged my hand upward and put my mouth around my fingers.

There was a hard knock on the door. With a sadistic smile, I turned toward the sound. I walked to the door and leaned my back against it. Enzo knocked so hard that it made the entire thing tremble behind me.

"Gia, what are you doing?"

"Nothing," I said through a moan as I rubbed between my legs again.

"So help me god, Giovanna, if you're doing what I think you're doing, the moment they find the damn key to this door, you will be sore and sorry for this stunt."

The pleasure warmed my belly as it rose, flushing my cheeks red. I moaned, which just hastened his attempts to get in.

"Get your hand off what's mine," he snarled.

"Yours?" I laughed.

"Even if *you* aren't mine, that pussy is fucking mine."

The door burst open, knocking me forward. Enzo's eyes were dark and fierce as he stepped into me. His hands whipped down my skirt, and his eyes dropped to my breasts, his lips tightening. He walked toward the center of the room and threw my shirt to me. "Put that shit on and get your ass over here."

I cocked my head at him. A tinge of excitement ripped through me. He was hard to read, and I was torn between wanting him to take me in his anger and leaving while I had the chance. I didn't expect him to play into my game.

I stepped toward him, expecting his expression to change into something I recognized. Instead, his face never lost its tension as he undid his belt and ripped it from the loops of his pants. I didn't move. I was too shocked by his anger to take another step.

He walked over, fisted my hair, and dragged me to the chair I'd used to tease him. He pushed me over, forcing me to grab the wicker arms as I leaned over it.

"Enzo . . ."

"Don't you talk sweet now. You wanna act up, play with my fucking head all over again? Nah. It ain't happening." His hands raced up my thighs and raised my skirt. Warm breath moved over the flesh of my ass as his hand ran across my skin. "I was out there for"—he looked at his watch—"five minutes, give or take. So you'll take five hits with my belt."

I scrunched my nose and made a move to stand up. "You aren't being serious."

"Be glad I'm not counting the whole time you were fucking with yourself. Bend over."

How bad could it be? I've been spanked. Shit, sometimes I even like it.

I wrapped my hands around the arms of the chair and braced myself. He ran the leather between my legs, my wetness soaking the surface, which would give the belt a bigger bite.

"If you lift either of those hands off the arms of the chair, I'm starting over."

I swallowed hard. I expected him to give me hard spanks, but not use the full strength of his arm as he drew the belt away and came down on my skin with a nauseating crack.

"One."

The sound separated the air, and the sharp inhale caught in my throat as I instinctively reached back and tried to baby the skin he'd hit. Enzo grabbed my wrist and put it back on the arm of the chair. He hauled his arm back and cracked the leather on my ass again. I arched my back in pain.

"One."

Fuck. I focused on keeping the muscles in my hands still, forcing them to stay wrapped around the wicker. He rubbed the belt between my legs again, coating it with my excitement once more before cracking my ass again.

"Two."

I bit my lip, trying to keep from screaming out. I wouldn't give him the satisfaction.

"I said I'd make you sore and sorry for playing with what's mine."

"I'm sorry," I said in a breathy voice, fighting the pain that still crawled along my skin, even in the belt's absence.

"You're never sorry," he said as he hauled his arm back and came down on me again. "Three."

My fingers rose from the wicker, but I kept my palms planted as I reminded myself to stay in contact with the chair. *Don't reach back. Don't move.*

"I told you I'd never cheat on you," he snarled as he came down on my ass again, harder this time, taking out his frustration on the sensitive skin. "Four. Everything I did was for you." He whipped me one final time. The hardest of them all.

I yelled out. It was too much to take so stoically.

"Five."

He threw his belt to the ground. Tears fell down my cheeks, and I wanted to wipe them away before he saw.

"Can I move my hands now?" I asked.

Enzo stepped in front of me and looked at my tear-stained cheeks. His hands reached out tenderly to wipe them away. He circled me again. "I don't know. You're dripping wet, even after all that."

"Fu—" I started to curse at him. But I caught myself. He was in a mood I hadn't seen before. At least, not directed at me. He had a sadistic side that came from a lifetime of pent-up anger. He was right, though. I thought I had been dripping blood down my thighs until I realized I hadn't been bleeding. I was so angry I was trembling, hating that I'd given him such power over me. But I was trembling from something more as well.

"I should fuck you and lean into those welts and bruises on your ass." His hand ran along my aching skin. I flinched at his touch. "You'd let me, wouldn't you?" he asked as he let his hand dip down and run along my pussy. I twitched. I ached for pleasure after such pain. He dropped his lips to my welts, kissing them. "I won't be doing that, though.

What kind of lesson would I be teaching you if I did? That you can do what I fucking *hate*, make a mockery of me in my own home, and still get to come?" Enzo circled me once more. "You're to keep your hands on the arm of that chair until I say you can let go."

"Why are you doing this to me?" I asked.

"Because when you refused to believe me, it hurt worse than any of this. I forgave you for infiltrating my family." He leaned low, close to my ear. "Shit, I forgave you for all of it." He swallowed hard. "I'm in a fucking nightmare, trying to somehow earn the trust of people whose loyalty I betrayed when I chose you over them. I'm choosing you yet again by even letting you be here. My life is going to be fucked if I let you stay here. And here I am . . . letting you stay here, allowing you to be in front of me again. I'm a goddamn fool."

"Enzo—"

"Save it, Gia. Stay. But those hands better not leave that chair, or I'll take up the bounty on your father my damn self."

My mouth dropped open. How could he say such a fucking thing? I exhaled as he left me ass-up to the camera, hands stuck to the chair's scratchy wicker. I was seeing the old Enzo, the one I grew up knowing the evils of, the person I forgot existed as he made love to me.

My ass ached. I wanted to reach back and touch my ailing skin, but I kept my hands firmly planted because *my* Enzo wasn't the one who just gave me that lashing, and I didn't know if whoever he was would make good on his promise. I shouldn't have pushed him. I knew Enzo would be overwhelmed after trying to worm his way back into the graces of people his business relied heavily on.

And what wouldn't help him gain grace was me.

Chapter Twelve

Enzo

I ran my hand along my revolver's slick metal as I cleaned it. The scent of gun oil filled the room. Atheist whined. "Shhh," I whispered as I wrapped a cloth around the barrel and rubbed it. It was much more sensual than I intended it to be, but I loved that damn gun. Atheist whined more forcefully at the door, and his sounds made me remember everything all at once.

Gia. The lashings. Making her stand like that until I came for her. I groaned, stood up, and checked the camera feed on my phone. She was squatting to take the weight off her arms, her hands still planted on the chair. Her dark hair flowed over her shoulder as her head dropped. I felt a pang of guilt. But just a quick one.

I left my room, comforting Atheist with a quick pat before I closed the door. My mind raced as I headed toward her room. She'd be pissed, and rightfully so, but I quite enjoyed seeing her obey for once in her fucking life. She'd submit to me any day during sex, but it wasn't true submission. No. Suffering through the ache of her hands and her arms was submission.

It was respect.

How she acted now would determine if I gave her the same.

I walked into the room and her head shot up, her back straightening, but she wouldn't look at me. I stepped closer and looked down at her tired eyes. Her hands trembled. I wanted to reach out and comfort her.

"Release," I said as I stood behind her head, rubbing my hands slowly from her shoulders down to her trembling wrists.

As soon as I gave her the word, her hands flew from the chair and she swung her elbow back and hit me in the dick. *Fair.* She ran to the bathroom, leaving me kneeling over the chair myself, trying to calm my anger. I wasn't surprised. I should have known she'd take a shot at me the moment she could. I shouldn't have served her my balls on a silver platter. I groaned. When I heard the water running in the bathroom, I stood tall and pretended there wasn't an ache in my nuts.

Gia came back into the room, her skirt pulled back into place, and curse words flew from her mouth as she rushed past me. "I'm leaving," she said, no argument in her tone.

"You aren't going anywhere, Giovanna." I matched the sternness in her voice. I was as sure she'd be staying as she was sure she'd be leaving. "There's nowhere for you to go. You've burned every bridge besides mine."

"Fuck you."

I pressed her against the wall, my hands on either side of her head. Fury glimmered in her eyes. I loved it. "It doesn't feel good, does it? To be hurt. See, I always knew you'd hurt me. You're a Silvani, after all. I should have known that love wasn't enough for two people like us. Hell, we might not even be capable of it. But I knew I wouldn't hurt you. Not like you thought I would. I might hurt this . . ." My hand jutted between her legs with a rough touch that made her gasp. "But I wouldn't have fucked around on you. I was fucking *obsessed* with you. There was no room for another woman, not even for a night." Silvio always cheated on my mother, and I vowed to never be that person. I never wanted to step a foot in the path Silvio came from. I forged my own. Her accusation of infidelity stung deeper than she realized.

She leaned in and kissed me, and I let myself kiss her back for a moment, bathing in the sweet taste of her lips. When her pelvis tilted against my touch between her legs, I tugged my hand away. No, she would *not* get what she wanted. Even if I wanted it, too. I needed to take my frustrations out on her body, but I couldn't forgive her. Not yet. I pulled away from her, and she whimpered as her lips chased mine.

"No, we ain't doing this," I said. When she reached for my pants, I grabbed her wrists in one of my hands and pinned them above her head. It only made her bite her lip, wanting more. I wiped at my mouth. "We ain't doing this. I can't keep you a secret, you know? You're coming to dinner with my brothers tonight, and I need you to not be so . . . you. Be someone who doesn't seem like they could have killed Silvio. Maybe a bit meek. A little ladylike."

"No promises," she said. "If you aren't going to fuck me, let go of my damn wrists."

I released her hands, and she dropped them to her sides and shook her head. I stepped away from her. "I'll have a dress sent up."

Dinner was going exactly how I expected. Sammy and Marco sat at the table, their faces red and angry as their eyes locked on Gia, who calmly took a drink of her water. Their glares burned through me, but they didn't seem to bother her. She couldn't care less if they stared.

"Marco—" she began, but the fierce snap of my brother's words nipped her sentence back.

"I have nothing to say to you, Ms. Silvani. I know you aren't his enemy, but you are *my* enemy."

"It doesn't have to be like that."

I kneed her beneath the table, trying to shut her damn mouth. She'd only fuel him. He hadn't drawn a gun on her yet, so dinner was going *better* than I expected at that point.

Sammy stabbed at his steak with aggressive motions that flung drops of red-tinged grease off his plate. There was silence except for the clang of forks against the ceramic. Over the soft groan beside me as Gia took a bite of her steak, her hand slipped beneath the table and between my legs. My lips tightened.

She better fucking not. My eyes leaped between my brothers, but they kept their eyes down as they ate.

"This is so . . . damn . . . good. My compliments to the chef," she said. The flirty tone in her voice even made Marco look up from his dinner. Her cloth napkin fell to the floor, and she kicked it further beneath it. "I'm so clumsy," she said as she squatted down and crawled beneath the table. "It's really dusty under here, boys. You guys should get one of those little robot vacuums. It would take care of all this for you." She spoke nonsense as her hands worked down my zipper and button. I tried to kick her away casually, without making a scene. She pulled me out of my boxers and kept her hand on my dick as she swiveled out from beneath the table. She kept herself angled just right as she scooted her chair closer to me and sat down with a huff. "Anyway, what were we talking about?" Gia looked around the room.

"More wine?" our waiter asked as I emptied my full glass into my mouth. I leaped as he approached, trying to keep him from seeing my dick and Gia's soft hand wrapped around it. I handed him the glass, pushing it across the table and away from my lap. He filled it with the deep red liquid and pushed it back before leaving through the double doors.

Gia stroked me. Her upper arm was motionless as her hand worked me. There was just a twitch of her biceps every time she stroked her hand around the head of my cock. I tightened my lips, flashing her a look that could kill. She just smiled back. I didn't like when she played my game.

"I don't know what kind of hold you have on my brother, but I don't trust your intentions," Marco finally said. She had a hold, all right. Her grip tightened on my dick.

"My words aren't going to mean shit to you Vigliones. All I can do is show you that I'm not the rival you think I am. I'm not my father."

I rolled my eyes. I asked her to behave for one night. My abdomen tightened as she increased her speed beneath the table. She was enjoying getting a rise out of me *and* my brothers.

"There's no family closer to each other than you and yours," Marco said. "You'd choose them over—"

"I haven't, have I?" she quipped, and I felt the heat of her glare beside me.

I took a shuddering breath as I closed my eyes for a moment to center myself, focusing on anything else besides the way her fingers moved along the ridges of me.

There was a panicked tightness in my gut as my brothers grew angrier. It intermingled with the pleasure between my legs. "Gia was supposed to record us when she was here, but she didn't." I kept my words steady as I tried to calm them down.

"I chose you fuckers over my own father," she said with a smile before stabbing her fork into the meat on her plate.

Just as I was about to come, she tugged her hand away and wrapped it around the knife before cutting into the steak in front of her. The sudden halt in pleasure made me swallow hard. I reached down and tucked myself back into my boxers and zipped my pants. My skin felt so sensitive as it rubbed the fabric. I didn't know if I was more upset with that stunt or the denial of pleasure.

My brothers sat back with a sharp exhale, as if they didn't know what to say next.

"So are you two fucking again?" Sammy asked.

"Hard no," Gia said with a laugh. "We're just friends, if you can even call it that." She tossed me a wink as she wrapped her hand around her glass and drank the wine in two big gulps. The waiter popped out, as if on cue. I shook my head at him. She didn't need any more wine. She'd pay for her behavior.

One way or another.

Chapter Thirteen

Gia

Part of me knew I shouldn't have done what I did. Having his cock in my hand again ignited a desire I tried to avoid. Teasing him made me feel powerful. He always had the upper hand when it came to who owned the pleasure. If I teased him enough, he'd take what he wanted regardless. And I'd let him. But beneath that table, when he was incapacitated, I almost made him come. I stopped before he could get a release, and that was delicious. I knew I'd pay for it, though. Oh, I'd pay for it.

Enzo didn't knock before he came into my room. His lips were taut and his steps showcased his frustration. I had removed my heels before he came in.

"Goddamn it, Gia," he hissed as he pushed me against the wall. The light switch dug into the middle of my back as he pressed his body into me. "What did I tell you before that dinner? I told you not to be yourself. Don't be Gia Silvani."

"How do you expect me to be anyone else?"

"I don't, and that's the problem. I also don't expect to have my dick stroked at a family fucking dinner." His eyes narrowed when a smirk crossed my face, and I gasped as his hand reached beneath my dress. With a harsh glare, he rubbed above my panties, the friction making everything feel that much more intense. My knees trembled, growing weaker with every caress. I reached out for him to steady myself, but he swatted my hand away. "You've touched me enough."

I knew he wouldn't let me come. I knew that the moment he came into this room. He'd never give me what I withheld from him. He'd stop me right at the cusp of my orgasm. When my toes curled over the edge of the cliff, he'd tug me back. Even though I knew he'd halt the brewing pleasure, I couldn't stop riding his hand. A devilish grin slipped onto his face because he knew what he was doing. He knew my body well enough to know that the curl of my pelvis meant I was getting close. I gripped my dress because I had nowhere else to grab. Every time I clutched his wrist, he pushed me away.

Just as I was about to come, he stopped and drew his hand away with a smirk. "Fuck you, Giovanna," he said in a low, seductive voice that made me melt.

"So we're back to this?"

He rubbed his hand down the front of my dress. "We ain't back to nothing. We can't be anything."

"We can't not be something, Enzo," I said with a voice that wavered at the end.

He shook his head. His eyebrows furrowed. The discontent was clear in his expression. Neither of us wanted this distance between us, a dark line that separated my blood from his. "Just let it go, Gia."

But I couldn't let him go.

Enzo

MY FAVORITE BAR downtown was ours. Well, one of ours. Ice cubes swirled around as I circled my rocks glass on the slick tabletop. It left a wet streak behind, following the path of my motion. The golden liquid reflected the bulb of light above it. I spun around in my chair and looked at the bar. Most of the patrons were one of us, and the rest were women who wanted to be with us.

The door swung open and in walked the force on heels that I neither expected nor wanted to see. Her dark eyes scanned the bar before she spotted me. Like a missile locked on its target, she made her way over to me. There wouldn't be anything to block her path.

"Hey," she said as she sat beside me.

"Ms. Bianchi."

"You can call me Senna." Her lips tightened.

Senna Bianchi was Bullseye's sister. They looked nothing alike, having come from different mothers, but both were crazy. She was small and had dark hair, but I could see the halo of red in the strands beneath the cool lights. She had Bullseye's wide-set nose, but those full lips definitely came from her mother. She always kept them pinched, making her look mean as fuck. She wasn't unattractive—quite the contrary—but she'd grab you by the balls and twist if she could get close enough.

"Enzo, you worked closely with my brother?"

Stay calm, I reminded myself. I never felt fear after a hit —or any murder, really—but I rarely had to sit beside the family of the deceased and lie to their face. "Yeah," I said, swirling my finger around the rim of the glass.

"I'm guessing you haven't heard from him, either?"

"Nah, I was out of the city for a while. He became a ghost while I was gone."

Senna ordered a drink, asking the bartender for whatever I was having. He came back and set down a clone of my drink.

Her eyes dropped to the sticky black tabletop. "Our soldiers found pieces of his dismantled car."

What she was saying made my heart skip a few beats, but I kept my eyes locked on the glass. "Why are you telling me this?"

She turned toward me and let her dark eyes pour into mine. "I want you to help me find out who killed him." She put her hand on my thigh. "Please."

She was looking her brother's murderer right in the eyes. Her hand was on the thigh of his killer.

I batted her hand away. "You don't know he's dead, Senna." I did.

"I know it. I can feel it. He wouldn't just leave."

"Things have been getting hot for most of us. Maybe he ghosted for a little while until things cooled down."

"My brother didn't run. He'd stay and fight."

That was true. In all my years of knowing Bullseye, he ain't ever ran.

"Come on, Enzo. You have the biggest eye on the city now. Can you at least keep it open?"

The way she looked at me, desperate and pleading, made me want to agree, even though I knew he wasn't ever going home. "I'll keep an eye out, Senna, but I got my own shit to watch."

Her eyes relaxed as she drew out a cigarette and lit it. I

watched her mouth, how it wrapped around the filter. Her cheeks sucked in as she inhaled the smoke.

"Can I have one?" I asked. Without looking at me, she pulled out the box and let me slip one out. She slid the lighter across the table. "I'll do what I can, Senna."

Her eyes jumped to mine. "That's all I ask," she said with a pinched smile. "Where's that Silvani girl?"

"We ain't together anymore."

A smile crossed her lips. "Why not? What'd you do?"

I shook my head and blew out smoke. "I didn't do anything. She *thought* I fucked with another woman."

Senna's eyebrows lifted. "You're one of the most faithful men in the city." Her lip twitched. "You weren't always like that, though. Remember when you used to say as long as it was just mouths and hands, it wasn't cheating?" She smirked at me.

I was young and stupid when I thought that, and Senna was once another woman. I fucked around on an old girlfriend with her, but I stuck to my mouth and hands and let her suck my dick at the club while I made her come with my fingers. It was so long ago that I'd nearly forgotten.

"We were young," I said with a shake of my head.

"It doesn't have to be something that happened so long ago," Senna said with a flirty rise in her brow.

I was tempted. I was *very* tempted. I still hadn't come since Gia stopped me. But there was no way I could fuck Senna without seeing her brother's bloated corpse when I closed my eyes. Nah. I couldn't.

"Not tonight, Senna," I told her. I wasn't completely shutting down her idea, but it was a soft no right then. I'd finish my drink and go home alone.

WHEN I GOT to the house, my brothers were smoking outside, with their eyes trained on the pool house. *What the hell are they looking at?*

Then I saw it.

Gia was standing in front of the wall of windows, wearing only her bra and panties. Her hair was slicked back and dripping wet.

I turned off the ignition instead of heading toward the garage and watched her, then my brothers. They hated her and still their eyes were locked on every curve. The slow, sensual way she moved as she reached back to unclip her bra made me fairly certain she knew she was being watched. Much too slow and sensual for a lone dip in the pool. My eyes dropped to the thin tan line that had been covered by her bra. I followed her body until I landed on her ass. It looked fucking incredible in her black panties. Bruises still peeked from beneath the fabric. The way her hips moved as she hooked her fingers into her panties and started to pull them down, I was certain she knew she was being watched. As the fabric rolled down half her ass, I slammed on my horn.

Gia turned around, clutching her bare chest. Her face had no fear, no embarrassment. My brothers scurried back inside. She knew what she was doing. She wanted to get my brothers going.

Alcohol swirled through my bloodstream, making it a bad time to confront her about it. *I'm not going to confront her,* I told myself as I got out of the car. *I'm just going to talk to her.* I made my way across the lush grass. Rainwater still clung to the tips of the blades, and it soaked through the bottom of my pants. Her expression shifted into something playful, and that was going to piss me off the moment I walked in there. *Just talk to her.*

I threw open the pool house door and walked into the potent scent of chlorine. Water beaded along the bottom of the windows from the steam and dripped toward the tile flooring.

"What's the matter?" she asked. Just like I thought, she was playing, and I wasn't in the mood to play.

"Are you out of your mind?" I snapped as I started to unbutton my shirt. I slipped it off and stepped into her, trying to ignore her perfect breasts as I put the shirt around her shoulders. "Cover up, for fuck's sake. What are you trying to do here? That show wasn't for me."

She shrugged. "Thought maybe it would help your brothers hate me less."

"They ain't gonna hate you less. They'll fuck you even if they don't like you, and you aren't all that likable, Gia. But you sure as shit are fuckable." I let the liquor talk as I looked at her in my dress shirt.

Her eyes rounded and her lower lip softly pouted. "Well?" she asked.

"Not gonna happen, babygirl," I said as I stepped into her and touched my forehead to hers. "I wish I could, but things are a fucking mess. Too messy for this shit. Whatever this is."

"Can't we not be enemies for—"

"Oh, don't start that. You aren't my enemy, you just can't be my ally. Not now."

"When have you cared what they thought about me? You let me come around them all before!" Her words rose sharply.

"That was before—"

"Before what?"

"Silvio, the hit on you, the ghosting," I whispered. "Bullseye."

"I didn't kill Silvio."

"I know you didn't. Now my brothers know you didn't, but what do you think they're gonna tell people? That it was you or your damn father. They ain't gonna say it was me. Even though it *was* me."

"Tell them all the truth," she whispered.

I rubbed my chin, smoothing down the hairs as I looked away. I met her gaze again. "You clearly are out of your damn mind."

I couldn't tell the truth without it ruining me. Wrecking the business. I could own it, crawl back to the top stronger than ever, but right now? The foundation was much too weak to come out with that kind of confidence. I'd fucking love to have Gia on my hip, destroying shit, merging families. I'd marry the fuck out of her and make her a Viglione. But the target on her back spilled onto me, even without me inside her.

Chapter Fourteen

Gia

I didn't want to stay here. I didn't realize how bad it would hurt to be around Enzo without being *with* him. How the fuck could we have a normal conversation when we were so estranged, so unwilling to push further? There wasn't anything more I could try. Asking him didn't work. Making him jealous didn't help. It sucked but I knew if the roles were reversed, I would have kept me at arm's length, too.

I walked down the hall and rubbed my hand along the big library doors. I pressed my ear to them, trying to hear if he was inside. He should have been in there, at his desk, doing boss-level shit. I knocked but heard nothing behind the doors. I pushed them open.

Enzo and his brother turned toward me with red faces and tight lips, as if they'd been arguing. He and Marco always seemed to get into it. Marco was clearly vying for Enzo's position. If it was purely from a business standpoint, he would be the better choice, not because he'd run things better, but because I had clouded Enzo's judgment. Even when he tried to hate me, he couldn't keep his mind off me. I could never run my father's business against Enzo. Not a chance in hell. I'd give up my empire for him in a heartbeat.

Their eyes remained locked on me like I was an intruder.

I was.

"This is what I mean. Fuck this," Marco said. He got to his feet and slammed his chair back before knocking into my shoulder as he rushed past.

Enzo stood, his posture rigid and protective. "Goddamn it, Gia. You have excellent timing, ya know that?" He dropped his hands to the desk in front of him and let out a groan. "Marco was just saying he worries about how much you'll intrude on business matters. And here you are, intruding."

I walked over to him and sat in the chair that Marco's heated presence just vacated. "I just wanted to talk . . ."

Enzo's eyes remained on mine, following my body as I sat. "About what?"

"This. Us."

He took a seat behind the desk, a smug look on his face. As he swiped his chin with his hand, I had never been more attracted to him. He looked so powerful. So strong. Exactly where he needed to be.

I had fucked up—I knew that—but instead of apologizing, I went all . . . Silvani on him. He deserved an apology, and I didn't deserve his forgiveness.

I leaned toward him. "What do I need to do? Beg?"

"I know how hard that would be for you." He spoke like he was my father. Condescending as fuck. And I liked it.

"I'm sorry, Enzo. I'm sorry that I didn't trust you. I shouldn't have . . . Jameson . . . I fucked everything up."

"Stop. You're all over the goddamn place." He stood and walked toward me with an overbearing presence. So tall and strong, amplified by the new position he held. This library was *his*. He fisted my hair, and my eyes fell to the pistol on his hip. He brushed a hand through my hair. "I can't stay mad at you for the accusation, or even for how it went down with Jameson. I've gotten over it. It's not about that, though. It's that we *can't* be what you want, what I want. This"—he gestured between us—"can't happen." A smile crossed his face. "But I haven't come since I was with you. If you want to apologize for playing with my cock beneath the dinner table, well, I'd allow that."

I bit my lip. It was a start. I knew once I made him come again, he'd want more. He'd need more. I made a move to drop to my knees, but he tugged me by the arm and dragged me to his desk, gesturing to the opening beneath it.

"Really?" I asked as he worked open his belt buckle.

"Get under the goddamn desk before I change my mind," he commanded.

The way he spoke made me fucking listen. I crawled under the desk and looked up at him as he sat down in the cushiony chair. He drew himself closer to the desk as I hid beneath it, between his thighs. I unzipped his pants and tugged out his cock. The silky skin felt warm and tempting in my hand. I wrapped my mouth around him with just a moment of hesitation. He felt so familiar against my tongue. He tasted familiar, too. When I swirled my tongue around his head, his noises lit up my memory. A groan slipped past his parted lips and made me flush with heat. I loved that damn sound.

"Enzo?" Marco's voice came back into the room.

I jumped beneath the table, thumping my head on the underside of the desk. Enzo grabbed me by the hair, his hand forcing me to stay where I was. His next words were spoken to Marco. "What's up?"

"What the hell did she want?" he said with a sneer in his tone as he sat down.

"To apologize." Enzo laughed.

"I'm surprised you didn't make her apologize with more than just her words."

I put my mouth around him again and ran my tongue along the sensitive ridge in the way I knew he loved. He made a noise that was some sort of attempt at muffling how it made him feel. Enzo shook his knee nervously as they stared in silence at each other. I took the opportunity to move my tongue up and down his length before taking him to the back of my throat. I tried to remain quiet and keep myself from gagging.

"Anyway, can we get back to what we were talking about before *she* interrupted?"

"Yeah," Enzo said with a short snap of the word. He grabbed the back of my head and tried to keep me from moving on him. I didn't know how his brother couldn't sense what was happening in front of him. Enzo's voice had a woven length of pleasure within its tone.

"I know I don't have a choice on whether she's here or not, but she's not one of *us*."

Enzo made a brief noise in response, and the way his thighs clenched showed me why he couldn't talk.

"I don't know what your problem is, but we gotta figure all this shit out. All that our father left behind. Things he didn't do. Things he fucking did that he shouldn't have done. It's all ours to sort through, and he didn't leave us a bit of intel. Disturbances are trickling in from all over the city. I thought that was what *you* were for, that you were the one advising him or at least knew who he'd talked to about his plans." Marco slammed his fist on the desk and it made me jolt.

Enzo would need to give a detailed response to this. I thought about pulling my mouth away from his dick to let him get it all out. Instead, I stopped moving my mouth up and down, but I didn't stop the movement of my tongue on his throbbing head.

"Silvio didn't tell me shit, and we ain't gonna find out what went to shit until it fully goes to sh . . . it." Enzo's voice quivered on that final word, and he extended his leg, shaking it. His hand reached for me again, trying to stop me. He knew I'd make too much noise if he tugged me off his dick, so he gave up, relaxing his hand into the mess of my dark hair.

"Sounds like a great fucking plan," Marco said, and I could almost hear the roll of his eyes.

"It's all we got," Enzo quipped.

Marco kept talking, and Enzo made every attempt to push him out. I tuned them out as much as I could and focused my mouth on him. The loud, spit-coated sounds in the enclosed box seemed to bounce off the wood. If Marco looked hard enough, he'd surely catch a glimpse of my bare feet beneath the desk.

"I can't do this with you right now, Marco!" I wasn't sure what preceded the rise in his voice, but I felt the tension rushing through Enzo's body.

"Fuck me for trying," Marco hissed. The chair squealed as its legs gripped the hardwood floors. Heavy footsteps receded. The door slammed.

"Fucking A, Gia." Enzo's voice was low and smooth again. "If I didn't make him leave, I was going to come right in your fucking throat in front of him." He groaned as he slid his chair back, made me crawl on my knees to him, and stood. I ran my fingers along him before taking him back into my mouth. "Do you know how hard it was not to come in your perfect little throat? Don't do that shit again. When I tell you to stop, you fucking stop." He slapped my cheek and sent a sharp burn crawling across my skin. "You know, it's been so long since I've gotten off, I kinda want to see how much I can give you."

I sat back on my heels. "What do you want?"

"I want to come on your pretty face. Good girls get it in their mouth, at the back of their throat where they hardly have to taste it. But you haven't been a good girl, have you?"

I shook my head. My pussy was so fucking wet, my excitement dripping past the thin fabric of my shorts and down my thighs. It didn't matter. He wouldn't touch me or let me touch myself.

Enzo groaned before shoving himself back inside my mouth. His hips pulsed against my face as he pushed himself deeper. He fucked my face until he gripped the base of his cock and pulled out of my mouth. He fisted my hair and craned my head back. I didn't close my eyes or react as he pumped his hand and came. The pearly beads rushed onto my lips and chin and dripped toward the curve of my neck. More shot up to my cheek as he rubbed it into my skin with his dick. Once he'd coated himself with his own come, he shoved it back into my mouth. I tasted all of him on the very tip of my tongue. I wiped what was left on my face onto my fingers and licked them.

"Goddamn it, Giovanna," he growled.

He'd need more of this. We both would.

Chapter Fifteen

Enzo

I thumbed through some paperwork as we sat in my car outside the dry cleaner's. This wasn't my damn job, but it became my responsibility. Silvio kept all his loan shark bullshit in a damn folder. He didn't believe in computers, said it'd be easier to toss that folder in a fire if we had to. He was probably right. I was trying to read through Silvio's chicken scratch and whatever the hell these clients were signing. Terms and conditions. How much they borrowed. It shouldn't have been my damn job—I had people to do it—but this family had blown off three of my men, and even Silvio didn't bother to go collect. Me? I was cleaning house, which meant getting these sneaky fucks to pay what they owed. Running away wouldn't erase their debt, much to their disappointment.

I blew out a deflated breath as I caught Gia out of the corner of my eye, staring at the business entrance with what I could only guess was longing. It was hard for people like us to stay out of the business. It was a life force of its own.

As I loaded my revolver, her eyes jumped to my gun as I handled the bullets. Her and that damn fetish. She fucked me with her eyes as I loaded each one. Well, fucked my gun. I regretted letting Gia put her mouth on me last night. I was weak. My body wanted her regardless of what my mind wanted, and she'd cornered me with that perfect mouth of hers. I closed the cylinder and tucked it into my holster. Her eyes followed my movement, as if in a trance.

"What are we doing? Someone in your position doesn't collect."

"No one else can collect from them. They've tried." I got out of the car. "You coming or what?"

"Yeah." She got out of the car and followed me.

A bell rang overhead as I opened the door, and murmurs swam around us. A shadow ducked out the moment they saw us.

Goddamn it. I didn't feel like fucking running today. "Gun on them!" I shouted to Gia as I ran through a doorway clad in thick rubber mats to stifle the sound from the back room. I rushed down a big hallway with loud machinery whirring around me. I felt like I was chasing a ghost. He fucking disappeared.

"Bro, stop! It's too fucking hot for this shit!" I yelled at the shadow when I saw it turn the corner. Sweat dripped down my back as I followed him. Dark doorways led to what I could only assume were closets. My eyes scanned the warehouse for the man. Yellow sludge dripped from the ceiling and slid down the walls. It smelled like clorox and soap, with a strong hint of mildew. The stale scent burned my nose. A cockroach crawled across the floor, and I stomped on it. Sunlight struggled to shine through windows caked with dirt and grime. Spots of them were covered in what looked like black mold. The longer I stayed there, the more my skin felt wet. Disgusting. "What was so worth saving about this damn place?"

As I got to the end of the hallway, I leaned back and exhaled. How the hell had I let him get away from me, too? Next time, I'd come in shooting. I didn't give a fuck. If he wanted to play stupid games, I'd give him some stupid prizes.

A broom clattered to the floor in one of the doorways on the right, and the glint of a silver watch pierced the dark room. I reached inside and grabbed the man's jacket, tugging him out. He screamed at me in another language.

"I know you speak English." I shook his jacket. "I don't know if this shit worked with my father, but it's not working with me."

Sweat poured down the man's temples. His thinning hair was brushed back and stuck to his scalp. He stopped flailing and speaking in his native language. "Fuck you," he hissed.

"Closer," I said as I drew my revolver and cocked it. "Why haven't you paid in three months? You ran from everyone else, but you ain't running from me. Pay what you owe, plus interest, and I have no more business with you."

"Mr. Viglione, please." His tone changed real quick, but his accent was still thick. "We don't have it. The economy—"

"Do I look like an economist to you, Mr. Chen? I don't give a flying fuck about the economy. I shouldn't even be here, doing this shit. We loaned you money for your piece of shit business out there, and I swear to god, I'll burn that shit to the ground with your fucking mother in it if you don't pay."

A gun cocked behind me, and my eyes narrowed before I turned my head toward the sound and peered down the barrel of a Glock. A young man with jet-black hair and high cheekbones stared at me. He looked no more than eighteen. He curled his finger around the trigger and told his father to get up in their native language. Mr. Chen scrambled to his feet.

"Fuck off." I grabbed Mr. Chen by the shoulder, pushing him back to his knees. I kept my eyes on the young man's curling finger. What was he gonna do? Shoot me? Fuck him.

The sound of another cocked handgun echoed through the warehouse. Gia popped up behind the young man, her pistol drawn on him. We were a centipede of goddamn threats. My eyes leaped to her, and her hip cocked, looking natural as fuck with her hand around that gun. She looked at home with that metal in her hand. I closed my eyes for a moment, reminding my dick that it was not the time. Also, that we hated her. We had to hate her.

"Gun down," Gia said. Her voice was calm and even.

"Him first," the young man gestured his barrel at me.

"I'm giving you fucks an opportunity to pay what you owe like men. You don't wanna pay? You ain't gonna have your business. You can't have both."

The wife showed up. Her small frame donned a green satchel that made her waddle as she walked. She tossed it on the ground, already open, showing bundles of cash inside.

"No!" her husband and the young man yelled in near unison.

"Go. You go!" She gestured at me with anger spewing from her pointed finger.

I uncocked my pistol. The young man dropped his. Gia kept hers up.

I scooped up the bag. "That wasn't so hard, was it?"

We left the warehouse through a back door. Gia kept a grasp on her pistol until we got to the car, and I tossed the bag in the trunk and closed it. My hand rode down her arm, gripping hers, which was still wrapped around the pistol. She flashed her eyes at me, dark and menacing, as if the excitement of what went down had breathed life back into her. This life.

If I didn't take her home I'd end up breaking my goddamn rule. I'd end up fucking her right then. She looked at me with such anger that it made my head swim.

"Put that away before you hurt yourself," I said.

She sneered and tucked her gun into her waistband. We got back in the car, and she crossed her legs, probably to hide how fucking wet that made her. She wasn't the only one aching about it.

"I told you to stay up front," I said as I kept my eyes locked ahead of me.

She brushed her hair over her shoulder. "Yeah, and if I'd listened, you'd probably be dead."

"He was a kid. He wasn't gonna do shit."

"You do know they have links to the . . . never mind. The Vigliones know everything." She dismissed me with a wave of her hand.

"Do you want me to drop you off at your pop's?" I asked. "Didn't think so. Stop being a bitch."

"You're lucky I don't want anything to do with your balls or I'd rip them off for that," she snarled.

She could lie all she wanted, but she wanted *something* to do with my balls. If she didn't, she wouldn't have been here under the guise of protection. Nah. I should have let her fend for herself, see how long she lasted amongst a family of targets, but as much as she pissed me the fuck off, I didn't want to see Gia dead. I did what I did to keep her stupid ass alive. I'd murdered Bullseye to save her, and I refused to let it all be in vain. Even if she was being a damn *bitch.*

We sat in silence as we drove back toward my home. Her fingers played along the plastic of the center console, an audible click with every pass of each nail.

"Thank you," I finally said.

She stopped moving her fingers. "You're welcome," she said before continuing the dance of her fingers.

How had we gotten to the point where we couldn't even talk to each other?

***

Gia

I ACHED. I throbbed between my legs with such tenacity that I felt almost sick. My stomach continued to tighten. It was heaven to draw my gun on someone again. Holding a life in my hand. Well, holding the means to take it, at least.

I wanted Enzo. I wouldn't tell him and give him the satisfaction right then, but I wanted him. All we'd have to do is break through the barrier between us, and the best way to do that would be for him to break through *me.*

I rocked my hips a bit as I sat with my legs clenched together. I rested a hand on my lap, putting pressure on the front of my pants, anything that I could grind into. Enzo kept driving, not paying me any mind. I moved my hips so subtly that had it not been for the parting of my lips as a moan rolled over my tongue, you'd never be able to tell what I was doing. It became harder to control the motion of my hips and the way my thighs tensed as I rocked. I was so close, though. So close, and I just wanted to get over that ledge and jump.

Enzo knew me so goddamn well. He spun the wheel and turned the car into a parking lot. I stopped moving my hips, letting myself bathe in the ripples of pleasure still coursing through me.

"What the fuck are you doing?" he snapped. He leaned over and tugged my hand away from my lap. "Your face is all fucking red. You think I don't know when you're going to come? After all we've been through? Fuck you," he snarled. "You have the brass balls to do it right beside me, in my goddamn car?" Anger radiated from him, painting his cheeks red.

"You owe me," I said.

Enzo cocked his head. "For what?"

"I made you come . . ."

"What are you, twelve? I don't have to scratch your back just 'cause you scratched mine."

"But I'm so fucking itchy, Enzo," I whined. I didn't mean to create such a pathetic and desperate sound.

"You think I ain't? I've been hard since you pulled your damn gun on that punk!"

I bit my lip, hoping he'd realize we both had a need. We were both needing a scratch. Nothing more, nothing less.

"Quit thinking what you're thinking. If I fucked you, I wouldn't let you come. I'd make sure *I* did, though. I'd come inside you while you were still aching for release. Don't fuck with me, Giovanna. I'm not in the mood."

I put my elbow on the armrest and dropped my head on it with a frustrated groan. The pleasure, while still rippling between my legs, was waning.

Enzo whipped out a lighter and lit himself a cigarette. He inhaled and exhaled, sending a curled wisp of smoke between us. It made the air feel stagnant. I reached my hand out for one, and he shoved the pack and the lighter into my palm and threw the car back in drive. Before he took his foot off the brake, he reached over and shoved my legs apart.

I was frustrated and annoyed as shit, but I could only think about how fucking explosive it would be when he finally fucked me. I almost didn't care if he let me come at all. I just wanted him inside me.

When we got back to his house, I climbed out of the car under his watchful eye. He followed me inside but instead of turning to go up to his side of the house, he continued behind me. Breath caught in my throat as his angry steps followed me and made me want to run, but I exhaled and lifted my chin. I refused to fear Enzo. He wouldn't touch me, not even in the way I wanted. He followed me into my room and slammed the door behind me.

"What the fuck do you want?" I finally asked. My body was wrought with tension from his silent anger behind me.

"I realized I was being unfair," he said.

"About?"

"Not letting you get off." Enzo raised his arm and flattened his hand against the wall beside my head as he pushed me into the wood. "You let me come on your pretty face." His words were molten slag, and I was melting. Enzo drew his phone out with his free hand and fucked around with it for what felt like an eternity before placing it on the table beside us. I looked at the blue screen and saw 2:00 inside a gray circle.

He wasn't being serious.

His dark, haunting eyes made me swallow hard as he stared at me and slid my pants down my thighs. He reached over and hit the start button. The clock started to count down. The moment it did, his hand was against me, palming me through my panties.

"You are fucking soaked," he groaned. "You have two minutes to come, or you won't be coming at all. Actually, one minute and fifty seconds."

I dropped my head back as he played me the way an expert musician plays an instrument he knows so well. He knew exactly how to rub me as he pulled my panties aside and circled my clit. I kept glancing at the clock as the time ticked by.

One minute thirty.

The more panicked I got about the time, the farther away my edge seemed to be. I was so damn wet, and I struggled to get close enough. I needed the friction.

One minute ten.

I moaned as I grabbed his shirt and drew him closer, hoping he wouldn't see the clock. Wouldn't stop me. The pleasure was building between my legs but not fast enough.

Fifty seconds.

He sank his fingers into me before rubbing me with his palm. "Come, babygirl, or you ain't going to."

Thirty-five seconds.

He looked devilish, the smile crisp on his face. He knew my body. He knew I wouldn't make it.

Fifteen seconds.

I tilted my pelvis and rode his hand, giving a final attempt at letting myself rip through my frustration.

Zero. The phone sang out. Time was up. Enzo stopped his motion. As he pulled out of me, I begged. "No, no, please, Enzo." I'd grovel at that point. I didn't care.

"Sorry, Gia," he said as he gave a final circle that made me jolt. "Time's up."

"Fuck you," I whispered. Then, unlike my orgasm, I

exploded. "Fuck you! Piece of shit. Goddamn you!" I screamed as I pulled up my pants.

"Yeah, yeah, I know I am," he said before leaving me angry and frustrated as fuck.

I considered running to the shower and rubbing out a well-deserved one, but I bit my lip and thought better of it. I couldn't prove it, but I was almost certain there was a camera in the bathroom . . . because he always showed up any time my hands wandered too far for too long, banging on the door like I was committing a goddamn felony. *Fuck him.*

Chapter Sixteen

Enzo

The sun's brutal rays forced my eyes to squint as I stepped out of the restaurant after a meeting. My shoulders tightened with tension. I had heard from a ratty little bird that the O'Rileys had their sights not only on me, but on Gia. Which was great, because that was just another bullseye on Gia's back.

I wasn't surprised. I knew it would happen. I always knew that the O'Rileys would wait until the right time to make their move. They'd wait till I built my empire up a bit and got comfortable before they struck me down. That's what I'd do, at least.

I got back in the car.

Gia was fanning herself in the passenger seat. "There's a law against leaving dogs in the car in this heat for a reason," she said.

"I cracked the window," I said with a smirk.

"Fuck you."

I turned up the A/C and took off for the club, which

was the last place I wanted to bring Gia. To protect her, I had to keep her closer than I wanted to. We didn't speak on the drive. She hadn't quite forgiven me for teasing her last night. She was just so damn fun to frustrate. She got so angry. So desperate.

It was fucking sexy.

By the time we got to the club, the redness in her cheeks subsided.

"Wait here," I told her as I got out of the car and leaned into her open window.

"I'll literally die if you leave me out here again," she said with narrowed eyes.

"Silvanis are like cockroaches. They don't die." I went to brush her hair back from her cheek, but she batted my hand away.

"Make it quick," she snapped.

I tapped the side of the car and went into the club. The stages were empty, though music blared loud enough to vibrate my chest. Men meandered around, getting drinks and waiting for the next girl to come out and perform for them. They were greasy fucks, the usual daytime trash that came into our club. I kept my least interesting women—the Tuesday Afternoon Crew is what I called them, no matter what day of the week it was—for these men. Women who were in the death throes of their lives as dancers. Was I a dick? Yeah, kinda. I wouldn't put Ashley—who couldn't stay clean off meth long enough to let the scabs on her face heal —on the stage during my best nights and weekends. I wasn't going to put Maria—two-time mom, possibly fucking pregnant again—out there, either.

My advice? Don't come to the fucking strip club at noon.

There was no DJ. The automated music system took

over in the afternoon. It sounded like goddamn elevator music between dancers, and it was horrible. I ignored the sticky floors beneath my shoes as I headed toward the back. The place had gone to shit under Silvio's control. It had been the best club within two hundred miles at one point. Now? You could find better girls on the street . . . probably.

I pushed open the metal door and it slammed behind me. I waved a quick greeting to the men bonding over the free booze inside. I would have loved to sit and chat. Socialize. Enjoy a drink. But I had Gia in the damn car, and I couldn't bring her in yet.

"All the drops go okay?" I asked the room as I squatted in front of the safe. I counted and signed off on the bundles of money, trying to figure out where Silvio had stashed some of it. Some here. Some there.

"Yeah, boss. Most of them," Vinny said after he cleared his throat.

My gaze shot to him. "*Most?*"

"There was a little incident. Hardly nothing." Vinny waved his hand dismissively.

"How much is it gonna cost me?" That's all I gave a fuck about.

"About fifty thousand if you're willing to write off a debt."

"And why would I do that?"

Vinny's hand rode along his tie. "Cause I killed the pops of the corner store on second . . ."

I stood up and cocked my head, trying to process what I heard as I walked toward them and put my hands on the table.

"Why would you kill anyone? You collect. If they don't pay, you tell me. If I can't get someone to collect, then we do what we gotta do."

"They haven't paid. I tried three times, I gave them three—"

I slammed my palm on the table. I didn't like people doing shit without talking to me first. It's called respect. "Did anyone see you?"

"Just the wife, sir."

"Then you know what you need to do, since you wanted to be so goddamn trigger happy. Think better of it next time you decide to shoot first and ask me later."

He needed to get rid of the wife. I wasn't putting that on any of my men. No, if he wanted to play boss, he could take the brunt of being a trigger-happy fuck. He was lucky I didn't shoot him on the spot for causing waves when I needed still waters.

"Enzo?" The metal door crept open. Kenny popped his head inside, his lips tight in a straight line. "You may want to come out here."

What now?

I followed Kenny out to the main club again. A slow, sensual song played over the loudspeaker, which meant that a dance was going on. I didn't care much to see who was dancing . . . until Kenny gestured with his chin.

My stomach tightened at what I saw. My jaw tensed. Anger rose, becoming the only thing I could feel. I used to think that seeing red was just a saying, but I was seeing fucking red, and my vision tunneled with the anger. My eyes were locked on the sensual swaying of the hips on stage. She'd lifted her skirt to show the cuffs of her ass, partially covered by red panties.

Gia.

Are you fucking kidding me? She sure knew how to piss me right the fuck off. She got on her goddamn hands and knees and crawled toward the slimeballs in the chairs in front of her. They slipped her bills, and she tucked them in her bra, thankfully still covered by her low cut shirt.

Her eyes met mine, and a sinful smile crept across her face.

Check-fucking-mate.

She sat up on her knees. Men cheered her on as she grasped the bottom of her shirt and started to lift it. The fabric got just above her navel before I was on her, ripping her from the stage. The men stood in protest, and I drew my gun and aimed at all four of them. When they threw their hands up and sat down, I holstered my revolver again and dragged her toward the front door.

"Why you gotta ruin the fun?" the bouncer said with a smile.

"Don't fucking start, Roy. I'll cut your eyes out for even looking at her."

I dragged her to the car and pushed her against the hot metal. She tried to take a step forward so the backs of her bare thighs wouldn't burn, but I pressed her into the pain.

"What the fucking fuck are you doing, Gia?"

Her eyes rounded playfully, as if she wasn't just showing her fucking ass to those goddamn men in there. She knew she'd won that round. Maybe even the whole goddamn game. "I didn't do anything," she quipped.

I sucked my teeth, trying to figure out how to control the anger that was about to overflow from me and onto her. My mind raced to all the ways I could punish her, fucking hurt her. I sure as shit didn't want to give her what she wanted. I thought about it, and I knew what I wanted to do. I'd regret it later, but fuck it.

She dug her heels in as I dragged her to the back of the club. Only a handful of the men remained. Gia lifted her chin as the door slammed and everyone turned to look at her. She went into business mode, smoothing down her skirt as their eyes remained locked on her.

"Why is *she* here?" Vinny asked.

"It's not your business," I hissed. I turned toward Gia. The jealousy fueled my anger, and that was exactly what her end game was. That's what she wanted to do to me because that would get her what she wanted. I stepped into her.

"Enzo, she was probably just playin' around. You were just playin' around, right, Gia?" Kenny said, trying to defend her.

"Don't," I snarled at him.

"I don't want to be a part of your dirty little sex games," Vinny said as he threw his chair back.

"I'll be a part," Antonio quipped with a smile. "She's a Silvani, but she looks like she tastes so damn good."

Gia cared about appearances and being respected for the bad bitch she was. Well, the bad bitch she used to be. She carved herself a place in the business despite being a woman, and I knew what would hurt her down to her core. It was something she sure as fuck didn't think I would do, even after she shook her ass on stage for some men. But I was fucking reckless when it came to her, and that was the problem.

I pushed her against the wall, encasing her wrists in my hand and forcing them above her head. Her eyes narrowed on me exactly how I hoped they would. Rage filled the voids inside her that made her think giving the patrons a show was a good fucking idea.

I heard the men talking behind me, but I couldn't decipher the words above my heartbeat in my ears. My hand rode up her thigh, drawing her skirt up. Her breath hitched, not from pleasure but from annoyance. The moment her red panties were exposed, some of the men yelled out for me to keep going.

Their excitement grounded me, and the gravity of what I was doing sent me crashing back into reality.

"Show's over," I growled.

Gia's breath heaved in her chest.

"But boss," someone said behind me.

I drew my revolver and turned to face them. "I said, show is fucking over. Get the fuck out." I raised my voice as I cocked my gun. Metal scraped against the floor and glasses crashed as the men scrambled to get out the door.

"Goddamn it, Gia," I snarled.

Her lips relaxed. "That wasn't my fault!"

"I can't think like a don around you. I make fucking mistakes. Like that." I gestured toward the door. "This is exactly why none of this can happen! And it *was* your fucking fault!" I dropped her wrists. "You fucked everything up when you went out there to dance. You think they weren't all gonna hear about it? Kenny saw it. The bouncer saw you." Anger swelled again.

"It was a stupid dance, Enzo. Why do you even care? You've made it clear that we aren't anything. That we can't be anything."

"Because you're mine, even when you aren't mine. No one else can look at your body like that," I said with my lips much too close to her fucking mouth. "I know what you're trying to do. You're using my possessiveness to get what you want."

Her lower lip jutted out in a pout that made me forget for a moment why I was mad at her to begin with. She was playing with my goddamn mind again. She wanted me to treat her like a whore. Not quite like this, but it was her end game after all.

I leaned a fraction of an inch closer to kiss her, hard and driven, as if I'd been thinking about her goddamn lips since the last time we kissed. Since they were last on my dick. She whimpered against my mouth as she kissed me back. I raised a hand to her throat, and she whimpered. That sound made me ache for her.

"I'll give in one damn time," I told her as I pulled away from her kiss. I'd give in because I needed it. I needed to come because I wasn't thinking straight, even more so than usual.

I tugged her over to the table and bent her over it. Her chest pressed against the aging metal and plastic, and her shirt absorbed the spilled alcohol. I unbuckled my belt and pulled out my cock. She backed into me as I pulled her panties to the side and pushed inside her.

It was heaven.

It was everything I tried to forget.

She felt incredible.

I pushed my hips into her as I buried myself to the hilt inside her. She moaned, dropping her face into the table and trembling as if she felt exactly how I felt. Her pussy clenched around me. I wanted to pull out. She didn't deserve to come. But I tried to pull out of her and she backed her ass into me, keeping me inside her.

"Please," she whispered.

I toyed with the idea. I wanted to feel her spasm around me as she came. Everything that had built up over the last few days. How bad her body needed the release. "Play with yourself, Giovanna. Make yourself come on my dick."

I stopped my hungry thrusts, leaving myself pushed as far as I could go inside her. My hands gripped her ass as she reached a hand down to rub herself. I wasn't going to make her come, no, but I wanted the benefits of her orgasm.

"Good girl," I whispered as she rubbed her clit. Her moans grew, becoming ragged as her breathing became heavier. "I want to feel you come around me."

"Please let me come," she begged, as if anticipating me stopping her. I wanted to, but I also wanted to feel her spasming around me. That need won out over wanting to edge the fuck out of her once more. I needed to feel how she tensed and tightened as she came. I wanted to ride out her spasms as I chased my own orgasm. I needed her to come so she'd stop acting up, testing me, and pushing every goddamn button I had. If I had to put her on my dick to get her off it, it was a sacrifice I had to make.

She came, hard. An earth-shattering orgasm that I felt through every fiber of my body. Her spasms tugged at me, and I met them with driven thrusts until I unleashed my pleasure inside her.

How the hell did she feel so right when we were so goddamn wrong?

Chapter Seventeen

Gia

Heat shimmer rose from the pavement as I waited in the car for Enzo. I had the windows down and my feet up on the dashboard. A door slammed and I turned to glance at the old factory Enzo had entered about a half hour before. I tugged the front of my shirt away from my sticky, sweat-slicked skin. When I saw his face, he looked annoyed, lips drawn tight. His hand wiped down his face.

I got out of the car, the cigarette dangling at my side. "You okay?" I asked.

He grabbed my cigarette and took a long drag. "Silvio just handled things . . . differently than I would have. He ran the business by bullying others. And no one trusts me."

"It'll come," I said as I tried to give him a comforting smile. I knew how hard it was to gain respect, let alone trust. We were mistrustful for a reason. It's how we kept out of prison. It's how we rose to the top. Trust got you caught or killed.

Enzo brought the cigarette back to his lips and inhaled.

His cheeks hollowed as he exhaled the smoke. "It's hot as balls out here."

"Yeah, tell me about it. You weren't the one waiting in the damn car," I said with a plastic smile.

"It was supposed to be quicker than that."

Enzo scanned the building. I followed his eyes and saw only a cracked window with a tattered piece of fabric swinging from it. His gaze lowered, checking every blemish on the building. The windows were mostly painted black or covered with plywood. I was surprised they even used it for business. It looked like it was about to fall down on itself.

"Something feels off," Enzo said as his posture stiffened. "The more I look at this place . . . I just don't think this is somewhere Silvio would have done business."

"Who set it up?"

"A bookie got in touch with my brother. Said he had been doing business with Silvio for years. I didn't see nothing in the office, but I couldn't find much in his mountain of paperwork."

"Did you recognize him?"

"Nah, but sports betting wasn't really my thing. Silvio loved the ponies, so I wouldn't be surprised if he was on our books, but it doesn't make sense."

Enzo's eyes kept rising and falling over that broken window where the tattered brown fabric played in the soft breeze. He squinted against the sun, and I tried to see what he was seeing. Enzo's eyes widened. He leaped in front of me, using his body to shield mine.

"Get in the car, Gia!" He shielded my movements as I got the door open. A suppressed gunshot fired, still loud as hell. It pinged against the pavement beside Enzo's feet. Another shot rang out as he slid across the front of the car and got into the driver's seat. A final shot came through the car panel just in front of my legs. I tucked my head, but bullets slice through cars as if they're made of butter. You learned that pretty fucking quick in this life.

My heart beat so hard against the wall of my chest that I thought it might explode. It roared in my ears as I kept my head low, with my hands around the back of my neck. Enzo released every curse word he could muster as he hit the gas and we got the hell out of there. Smoke rose from the front of the car where a bullet hole had pierced the hood. Sun shone through a hole in the side panel beside me. As much as I'd been shot at, it never stopped humbling the fuck out of me. It had a way of putting things into perspective.

His eyes were wide as he reached out for me. He swerved into a parking lot, and I lifted my head. "Are you hit?" he asked, prodding at me to move my legs. "I think it was a .50 cal. Pretty fucking excessive." His lips curled. "This is real fucking bad, Gia."

I tried to force the rise of my chest into a more natural speed. It had been a while since I was shot at like that. "Do you think that's who shot Atheist?"

"The ones who shot Atheist were amateurs. This was not."

"O'Rileys?" I asked.

"Possibly. I expected more of a warning if they were coming, though."

"Maybe that was the warning?"

"It could be them. It could be any one of the people who slapped a target on your back," he snarled.

"Don't take this out on me! I didn't shoot Jameson. Or your damn father, for that matter."

"Yeah, yeah. Trouble follows you, babygirl. I'll go talk to my brother. Fuck . . ." he said as he watched the smoke rising from the hood. "This draws attention where I don't want it."

I looked around the open parking lot. "I know someone who can tow the car. Want me to call him?"

He pulled the keys from the ignition and tossed them on the dash. I got out of the car and made the call to Zane's Towing. He was known for his sketchy tows and little else. If a vehicle was being towed by Zane, it was probably because of something illegal. Cars, trucks, RVs, shit, even boats. I told him where we were and hung up.

"Now we wait," I told Enzo as I drew out another cigarette and leaned against the hood.

We waited in thick silence until Zane's fancy tow truck came whirling into the parking lot. He pulled up beside us, lifting aviators to look at us. "Am I seeing straight? A Silvani and a Viglione? Together?" Zane said with an exaggerated expression of surprise. He opened the door and stepped down to the ground. "Who'd you two piss off?" he asked as he put his hand by the bullet hole on the hood. The frayed metal curled inward.

"Do we not pay for your discretion?" Enzo asked.

Zane threw his hands up. "Yeah, I guess." He looked at me and smiled. "Giovanna Silvani, how the hell are you?" he asked as he stepped into me and gave me a hug. "How's your pops?"

"Do we have to do this here?" Enzo said.

Zane had been on our family books for as long as I could remember. Enzo didn't need to be jealous of him. He was like an uncle to me. It used to give my mother a heart attack when he'd toss us onto his lap on a new motorcycle and take us for a ride. Me and Ro were lucky to make it to adulthood. He had a good heart, though.

"Where you want it, boss?" Zane turned toward Enzo.

"Dump it. Do anything but bring it back to the damn house."

"You want it scrapped?" Zane asked as he rubbed his hand along the once-perfect exterior of the BMW. "That hurts my heart."

"If you wanna keep it, just get all traces of me off the damn thing."

Zane nodded and worked to get it loaded up behind his truck. He secured it and walked over to me, sticking out his hand. "Nice seeing you again. You all have been too quiet lately." He pivoted and stuck his hand out to Enzo, a pained expression on his face. Enzo shook his hand and Zane got in the truck and drove off.

Enzo and I looked at each other. "Cab?" I asked.

"Marco's coming. I already texted him."

"Fantastic," I said with more sarcasm than I intended to show.

We sat on the curb, in the sweltering fucking heat, waiting for his brother, who took his sweet time. Sweat dripped down Enzo's temples as he sat in deep thought. My sweat dripped between my tits. He had shed more and more clothes until he was wearing nothing but his slacks and white sleeveless shirt. I stared at his taut, angry muscles glistening with sweat, and I had to remind myself to pick my jaw up before he saw me staring. I thought about how he stood in front of me. Protected me from the gunfire. I swallowed hard and looked away.

An SUV pulled in front of us. Marco looked as friendly as I expected as Enzo got in the passenger seat and I got in the backseat.

"What happened?"

"Ask me when I'm not so angry or overheated," Enzo said.

"What about you?" Marco shot me a glare through the rearview mirror.

I shrugged. I had no clue what the hell happened. I wasn't involved in setting that whole thing up. In fact, Marco was. He should have known better than all of us.

"Who set this up?" Enzo finally asked.

"I told you. That bookie. Reno, or whatever his name was, said he worked with our pops. He wanted a meeting set up with you."

"What did he sound like?"

"I don't know, Enzo."

"Did he have a real deep voice?"

"Nah, he definitely did not," Marco said with a quick shake of his head.

"Remember what I told you about the O'Rileys?" Enzo asked Marco.

"Are you about to say something that's gonna piss me off?"

"Yeah. I fucked up," Enzo began. "I killed the oldest son."

Marco nearly swerved into traffic at Enzo's confession. He jerked the wheel to straighten us out.

"Are you serious?" Marco asked, staring at me through the mirror like it was my fault. It was very indirectly my fault, but it was mostly Enzo's.

We had to enjoy the quiet for the moment because a storm loomed on the horizon.

Chapter Eighteen

Enzo

I ain't ever been afraid of death, and facing it only made me angry. I'd been shot at plenty. So why was I so shaken up? I dropped my face into Atheist's neck, inhaling his scent. Like grass and dirt. He whined as I leaned against him. There'd been so many times I sat exactly like this, pouring my weakness into my goddamn dog. My best friend. I knew why I was so shaken up, but I didn't want to admit it. Everything inside me fought against it.

Don't even think about it. Let it go. Let her go.

Fucking Gia.

I had worked so damn hard to put distance between us. I let her go. The space would have eventually dissolved the ache until it became a dull throb. I kept telling myself we couldn't be together because she didn't trust me, but I knew the real reason. How could I run the business with her on my dick? I couldn't. Then I found out she was shacking up with fucking Rosario, and I was done thinking with my rational head. All I could think about was her riding his cock or taking all of him inside her perfect mouth. I imagined his pleasure, because she was the most incredible source of it. I longed for it. I fucking needed it. A guy could only take that plaguing thought for so long. I was going to take her away from him and put her somewhere safe, under my watchful eyes. The problem with my plan was that I couldn't keep myself from watching her. Salivating over her. It was fucking pathetic.

I glanced at my phone—one of the ways I kept tabs on her. She had the nerve to touch herself, knowing all too well how much it'd fuck with me. I wanted to be the fingers stroking between her legs and slipping inside her. The soft moans that left her lips should have been from pleasure I created.

I felt a pang of guilt over what I did to her—the whipping. I remembered the sound my belt made as it cracked across her perfect ass. I didn't *like* hurting her, but she had swung through every round of my patience. Even as tears fell and she actually listened for once in her fucking life, I didn't *enjoy* her submission. I liked Gia's fire, her drive, as annoying as it was. I didn't like feeling her genuine fear. It was something I'd never faced, not as I threatened to take her sweet pussy, not when guns were drawn on her. I saw a glimpse of it when Lorenzo did what he almost did to her or when she found out about the hit on her father. I felt it smoldering around her, but it wasn't the same.

It wasn't fear of *me*.

But there was something else there. The fear, the punishment, her anger—those things warped into something that dripped down her thighs with every crack of the leather. An uncomfortable push and pull of desire and hatred that fragmented us that night. I was fighting it so damn hard. As hard as I could.

When the gunshots rang out, I could only hear the beat of my heart slamming against my eardrums. It was a roar, drowning out everything else. Despite the disorienting thumps of my heart, I needed to protect Gia. Not myself. Gia. It was at that moment, as I threw my body in front of her to shield her from bullets, that I realized Gia would have to be dead for me to stop needing her. She'd have to be buried to keep me from thinking about her. What she was doing. Who she was doing. If she was fucking safe.

Atheist panted, his sides expanding against mine as he grew restless. I looked up, following where his dark eyes had fallen on something that made him wag his little nub of a tail.

Gia.

She stood in the doorway, and I don't know how long she'd been there or how much she'd seen. I wasn't allowed to be weak around others, only Atheist, who couldn't speak about it. That damn dog knew too much. He knew all my secrets.

He whined again, and I smirked as I rubbed his massive head and let him leap off the couch. He rushed for Gia, slamming all his weight into her as she squatted down to greet him.

I sat back on the couch and gathered my composure. I had to. My first instinct was to push her away. My second was to draw her into me and kiss her like it would be our final embrace. I decided against speaking because I wasn't sure I could control what came out, in either direction.

"Sorry to barge in," she said as she gripped Atheist's ear and stood up, letting the velvet fur fall out of her grasp. Her eyes met mine. I couldn't read her. She was probably fighting her instincts, too.

"Come here," I said, letting my second instinct take the lead.

She hesitated. Her muscles twitched as if she was going to come toward me, but they relaxed in place.

"Don't make me ask twice, Gia." My voice was stern, with growing agitation as my first instinct closed in. She was going to determine which one would win. I was giving in, extending the whole damn olive tree. *Your move*, I thought to myself. One of us had to give in order to take.

Just as my first instinct was about to rip through the ribbon at the finish line, Gia stepped forward and sat beside me, burying herself into my chest, much like I did to Atheist. I didn't move my arms from the back of the couch as she wrapped her arms around me and clung to me. The moment I felt the heat of her against my body, my second instinct cut the legs off my first. It had no chance of making it to the end now.

My muscles twitched, wanting to wrap her up in my arms, but I kept still, forcing them to stay where they were. I shed my hesitation as I lowered my arms and wrapped them around her. She melted into me. I didn't know what all this was. Was it all because of the shooting?

Gia

I LISTENED to the rhythmic beat of his heart. His soft t-shirt rubbed against my cheek. I didn't want to let myself be weak or fall into his lap like that, but I found myself needing him and growing tired of fighting it, of fighting him. I just wanted to forget about it all for a little while—the O'Rileys, Bullseye, and his goddamn brother.

And the shooting.

I wanted to pretend it was just us again, at that nice little house upstate. I imagined we had the hardwoods beneath our feet instead of the carpet, the open yard outside the door instead of gates and guards. I longed for something we'd never have again. Even if we could somehow get past the tug-of-war between us, it wouldn't work. I was a Silvani. Enemy number one and a threat to his empire. What could we ever be?

Despite knowing how futile it was, I melted into him as each breath made his chest rise against me. Putting distance between us was easier said than done. There was a relentless, toxic tug toward each other.

Fingers brushed through my hair, pushing strands away from my face. They left my head and grasped my chin, raising it up to face him.

"We're making a goddamn mistake," he whispered.

"We aren't doing anything," I corrected.

"I've already begun to fuck you in my head." His words were so low and laced with hunger that it made me throb between my legs. Every syllable went straight there.

He pushed me onto my back and climbed over me. His mouth dropped to mine and spread roughly over my lips. His hand rode up my side and grazed the crook of my neck before lacing behind it. His other hand worked down his sweatpants. As he pulled himself out, I slipped my shorts off without breaking the kiss. I worried he would stop us, and I thought about stopping it myself, but I needed it as much as my next breath.

He spit in his hand, rubbing it on my pussy before palming himself and pushing inside me. He growled against my mouth as he pressed his hips into mine so I could take all of him. I gasped as he sank as deep as he could inside me.

"Big fucking mistake," he said with a groan. "Worth every goddamn second." He spoke the words into my mouth as he kissed me harder, and my back arched beneath him. His strong arms flexed beside my head. My chest rose to meet his as my moans poured out from between our lips. "I love those noises, Giovanna. I—"

He stopped himself as he drew his hips back before pushing deeper into me. His skin clashed against mine. I whimpered as he leaned down and bit into my shoulder. His cock twitched inside me at the sound. I was hung up on what he stopped himself from saying.

"Say what you were going to say." I moved my face from his, and he stopped his thrusts and stared at me. His fingers grazed his chin, leaving a smirk on his face that made me melt into the couch. The look on his face said he wouldn't tell me. Instead, he jerked his hips forward and made me scream out. I forgot all about the lost words as he pushed into me.

His hand reached down and rubbed my clit, and electricity jolted through my body. I had craved his touch so much more than I realized. I moaned into the air and when I looked at his familiar, sadistic smirk, I knew what was coming, and it wasn't me.

"You know I'm going to bring you real close, baby girl. That's it. Bring you right to the edge and hold you over it."

I pouted. I almost pushed him off me and told him to go fuck himself. But as his fingers swirled around my clit again, I let him take me for the ride up, knowing he wouldn't let me down. I clenched around him as I got closer and closer. He stopped every time, so in tune with my body, which was fucking annoying.

"Please," I finally begged. I couldn't take the buildup and letdown any longer.

"I told you, no. If I have to, I'll pull out of you and come all over your pussy," he growled as he brushed his thumb along my clit. I jolted.

Every time, I thought he'd miss the mark, that he'd push me just a little too far, that he'd accidentally let me fall, but he always stopped just as my body was about to reach my apex of pleasure. He'd hold still, draw his hand away, and push his fingers into my mouth. Sweat beaded and dripped down my temples. It was so damn frustrating.

"Every time I edge you . . . I edge myself. I'm so close. I just want to spread your legs wider and fuck you mercilessly until I come." His eyes roved over me, stopping at the swells of my breasts. "But I know that would make you come. I can feel it."

I went to reach my hand between my legs, but he pinned my wrists above my head. The way he leaned over me put pressure on my clit, and I moved my hips subtly beneath him, just a minor tilt in my pelvis, back and forth. As he fought for my hands, with his cock buried deep inside me, the friction was enough to throw me off the edge. I shuddered beneath him as I finally got a release.

Enzo's eyes narrowed and his hand dropped to my throat. He squeezed, lifting me up so that I had to reach back to keep from choking. "I didn't say you could come," he snarled. His words were breathy, as if he were riding the waves of my orgasm around his dick.

"You can only tease someone so much," I choked out, my cheeks flushing with heat.

He drew a frustrated breath, sat up, pulled out of me, and flipped me onto my belly. His hands raced down my sides before gripping my ass. "Perfect fucking ass," he groaned. He rubbed his cock against the excitement nearly dripping from between my legs. Once he coated himself in my slick wetness, he pinned me beneath him and edged his dick into my ass. I reached back to stop him, but his tip was already inside me, stretching me. I gasped. The pain was too much to let me choke out the word "stop." But part of me didn't want him to stop, and that held the word in my chest.

A slow and purposeful groan left his lips as he pushed into me, and I shivered. Heat crawled along my skin, and I fought back tears that tried to fall out of pure instinct.

Enzo brushed my hair off my face. "That right there," he whispered, "is why I fucking love you, Giovanna." I tensed at his tone, which just made him groan as I tightened around him. "You always get what you want. Somehow, someway, you get the upper hand. You don't have the upper hand right now, babygirl, and you have no way to get it." He pinned my arms above my head. He was right. As electrified as my pussy still felt against the fabric as he thrust slow and deep inside me, I was still beneath him. "But that's why we won't work."

Now he'd made me fucking angry. I let him inside me, in a way I never had, and he felt the need to tell me why we couldn't be together. I fought the pain with the pleasure from how big he was, all for him to tell me he didn't want to be with me.

"Fuck you."

Enzo gripped my hip and squeezed. "You didn't let me finish," he said before kissing the back of my shoulder—a tender touch that countered the rough one. He drove his hips into me, slow and shallow, as he chased his pleasure. "I said it's why we won't work. But there's no other option but to try to make it. I will step down from my position if I have to. I can't focus, whether I'm with you or without you . . . and I'd rather be with you. We're either going to break down our family rivalry or cause a goddamn war."

Enzo fisted my hair and craned my neck. He was so deep I thought he would rip me open. He pulled back enough to quicken his thrusts before they grew ragged. He came inside me, with a gravelly moan that was so satiated with pleasure I felt it in my pelvis.

We were making a mistake, of course, but it's what we did. I'd know in the morning if he meant what he'd said or if he'd push me as far away as he could. Maybe further than ever.

Chapter Nineteen

Enzo

Gia was still asleep. I lay awake with my thoughts running all over the damn place. Atheist slept between us, snoring away. I was the only one who was restless. I kept replaying what I said to her, that I would give up everything to be with her. Could I? Would I be able to?

My position was something I had worked my whole life for. I'd done things for Silvio I'd never forget. Would I let it all go for someone like her? I wouldn't if we stayed this toxic together. The push and pull? We'd always have that, especially when I continued to edge her like I loved to do. But love had to lie beneath that moment of hatred. I had to be sure of that.

Maybe we'd both get our shit together, and I wouldn't have to give up a damn thing. Have my cake and eat the fuck out of it, too.

Gia rustled beside me, but she stayed asleep. My thoughts returned to last night and how I'd let my anger get the best of me, yet again. I made her take me in a way I'd never asked her to. We hadn't even discussed it, and I knew I'd hurt her. We took a shower together after, but she was so withdrawn and quiet, which was very unlike her. I just wanted to punish her for making herself come. The worst part? I hadn't doled out the actual punishment for that. I knew exactly what I was going to do to her.

So what was last night if not her punishment? It was selfishness. I wanted to feel her ass around me. I wanted her to hurt, to be scared. She wasn't scared, though. Surprised? Yeah, more surprised than anything. She was more hung up on me telling her I loved her than she was about me burying myself in her ass.

Fucking Gia.

"What time is it?" she asked as she turned onto her back, startling me from my thoughts.

"Ten thirty."

She yawned. "Why'd we sleep so late?"

"Well, I was balls deep in you until three a.m." I smirked at her.

"About that," she said as she turned toward me. I expected her to be all Silvani about it. I was waiting for the lashing she'd give me with her tongue once she found her voice. "I don't care if you fuck my ass. You know I'd give you anything. But I wish we'd had a conversation about it first." She swallowed hard. "Do you know what men who have raped me really loved? To fuck me in the ass. They get off on the pain, and they don't have to worry about knocking you up as they come inside you."

My heart sank. I hadn't considered her past as I turned her over and forced my way inside her. She didn't care when I forced my way into her pussy, and men had taken that from her too, which meant they were worse with her when they fucked her ass. That's what she hung onto. It was part of her past she locked away from me. I was a dick for not thinking about it.

She blinked away the gloss in her eyes. "Don't pity me, Enzo. It's fine. I should have told you to stop."

I tensed. I wasn't sure I would have stopped if she asked me to. I would have thought it was like every other time. Her stops were usually soft, not hard. I pulled her into me, brushing a hand through her thick, dark hair. "Do you want to talk about it?" I asked.

She shook her head but started speaking anyway. "There were the three men who collected on a debt once. All three took turns fucking my . . ." Her words broke off. In Gia fashion, she let her weakness slip away and she donned a hardened mask. "All three fucked my ass."

I didn't regret causing her pain or fucking her like that, but I regretted not giving her a chance to tell me her story. "I wish you'd tell me the names of the men who've hurt you, Gia."

"No, because you'd go all Viglione on them, and I couldn't forgive myself if something happened to you while defending honor that's been long gone."

She was right. I'd have killed every single one of the men who'd hurt her, then I'd have served their dicks to her on a silver fucking platter. The roots of her pain grounded her, but she didn't want to punish the monsters who planted it inside her. She was a better person than I was. I took revenge the first chance I got. I ripped my pain from the ground and burned it. In some ways, we were the same person, but I could never be as strong as her.

Guilt hung over me like the blanket wrapped around her shoulders. I'd like to think I would have stopped, but part of me would have wanted to keep going so she could come again with my dick in her ass, make her forget about the pain of her past, because I knew that would help her move on. Replacing her pain with my pleasure calmed the beast inside her.

"I'm sorry, babygirl." I tugged her to my mouth and kissed her. "Next time I'll make you come from my cock in your pussy, then I'll make you come again as I fuck your ass."

Then she asked what I'd hoped she wouldn't. "Did you mean what you said last night?"

"Which part?"

"Which one were you lying about? If it was all true, you wouldn't need to put it in parts."

"I meant it when I said I loved you. I was possibly lying about giving up my position. I'm hoping I don't have to make that choice."

"Haven't you kind of had to already?"

"Not explicitly. Logistically, I don't know how the *fuck* this is going to work. But I need it to."

"And if it doesn't?"

"I'll kill what doesn't make it work," I said with an eerie calmness. She needed to stop prying. I'd killed for her. I'd kill again for her. She knew that already.

***

GIA and I went down for breakfast. Lunch? Brunch? Whatever the fuck it was, I was starving. I smirked as Gia walked ahead of me. Honestly, she walked like she was *thoroughly* fucked last night. My lips tightened when I thought about the possibility of meeting my brothers in the kitchen. Would they be able to tell that subtle tic in her step was from being used to the point of soreness? Goddamn.

Regardless, I liked to see it. I missed it. We hadn't woken up together in quite some time.

Gia made it to the island first and plucked an orange from the bowl on the counter. She worked at peeling it open. Sammy looked up from his laptop to watch her. His eyes scanned her, examining her. I couldn't tell what he was seeing, but I didn't like the look on his fucking face from what he saw. She was oblivious to his staring as she tossed the peels into the trash. When she finally looked up, he snatched his gaze away from her. I hung around her protectively as I picked at some breakfast. I wasn't sure if he was looking at her the way I looked at her—like I couldn't wait to sink my teeth into her—or if he was plotting her demise. I wasn't okay with either option.

There was no hiding that I fucked her. We came downstairs together and she was wearing my t-shirt over her short shorts. She *looked* fucked. And she acted like it, too. Calm. Complacent. Satiated. At least until she became ravenous and went out of her way to fuck with me again.

Marco walked into the room. "Sammy, there's fifty large missing from—" He stopped when he finally looked up and saw us in the kitchen.

"Missing from?" I asked.

Marco's eyes leaped from mine to Gia's and finally landed on Sammy. He didn't want to talk business around her, I knew that, but if I had any hope of making this work, he needed to get used to it. "M-missing . . ."

"For fuck's sake, Marco, spit it out."

He cleared his throat. "From one of the off-shore accounts."

"Is it missing, or is this the result of poor record keeping? Because I have little faith after seeing how he kept track of shit."

"I don't fucking know, Enzo. I don't know. It says there should be two-seventy-five, but there's only two-twenty-five." Marco's free hand gestured while the other held the paper. A red blaze of frustration popped onto his cheeks.

"Silvio probably sniffed that away," I said with an annoyed snap in my tone as I sat at the table.

"Our father didn't—" Sammy shook his head, stopping his own sentence. His naivety floored me. They had no idea Silvio did coke and used family money to support his ever-growing habit. At the rate he was going, he would have spent all our damn cash in another ten years. There were going to be holes in accounts because of it. I had to use money to get him his dope, and I sure as fuck wasn't using any of my own to support his ass. But that's where the problem would lie. I wasn't sure what accounts he'd drawn money from. A little from several, if I had to guess. I just knew he handed me money, and I went and got him his drugs. I doubt he left a trail to follow, so if shit was missing, it was probably from that, but there'd be no way to know for sure.

"We need to stop looking for discrepancies, alright?" I snatched the paper from Marco and ripped it up. "Silvio was a god-awful book keeper. I say we focus on what we have and where. Forget about what it *should* be. It is what it is. There's no point in hunting cash we ain't gonna find."

"Alright, then I guess Sammy should balance the books," Marco said.

"Why me?" Sammy asked.

"Because you got great attention to detail." I seethed the words, and he knew I was talking about the way he'd stared at Gia. He cleared his throat, cheeks flaming red as he swept his laptop off the table and left.

Gia ripped pieces of her orange apart and ate them. "I

can help with the books. I used to do it for my dad." She pulled her legs beneath her.

"Not—" Marco snapped.

"Maybe," I interrupted.

"Did you guys check sub-accounts?" she asked.

"No—"

"I'm sure he—" We responded over each other. I cocked my head at Marco. "You haven't checked sub-accounts?"

"I . . ." Marco looked back toward where Sammy had gone, and I expected him to run off, too. Not only was he not looking at the extent of the accounts, but it was Gia, his nemesis, who pointed it out. How embarrassing for him.

"Just go find them," I commanded.

Marco left me and Gia alone in the kitchen. She stuck the final piece of orange into her mouth, the sweet juice dripping down her chin as she bit down. She looked smug, as she should. Marco should have known that. Her dark eyes sparkled with pride. She wiped the juice off her chin with the back of her hand. If she kept up shit like that, she'd be an asset to the damn business.

Our business.

Chapter Twenty

Gia

Enzo told me to meet him on the balcony at seven. He left me another letter like the first time. Memories flashed through my mind of one of the first times he edged me. It was the most frustrating memory. Even then, I was weak over it. Memories replayed after that, all the push and pull between us since, but I never doubted how much Enzo cared about me, even as he was pissing me off by playing with me and my mind.

I watched the clock from my room. The minutes passed slowly. I looked at the box he left me and knew what would be in it. Something he wanted me to wear for him. It all felt so eerily similar. I got up and grabbed the box, opening it as I walked back to the bed.

It wasn't a long fancy dress like he gave me last time. It was a shorter dress in a deep shade of purple, like his favorite dress shirt. I scrunched my nose. Wasn't quite the date dress I expected, which made me wonder what Enzo had in mind.

I undressed in the bathroom and slipped it on. The hem landed at mid-thigh, fitted from the top to the bottom, as if he had it custom made. It hugged my curves, and the neckline plunged, showcasing the swells of my breasts. I groaned as I took it all in. I didn't know what Enzo had planned, but I already knew I wouldn't like it. Was it my punishment for coming? It couldn't be. He already took my ass for that transgression.

My dark hair hung limper than I would have liked. I pinched it up in a clip, letting loose pieces fall and frame my face. A bit of dark makeup perfected my look. It was the best smoky eye I could pull off. The more I did myself up, the more I looked like a well-paid escort.

The clock struck seven. I put on my heels on my way out the door and headed toward the balcony, passing Enzo's men on my way. My cheeks flushed with heat, and I tugged at my dress, trying to cover myself. It was futile.

I gripped the balcony door's cold metal handle and sucked in a sharp breath before opening it. The moment I stepped out, before I could speak, Enzo wrapped his hand around my mouth, smearing my lipstick.

"Shh," he whispered as I writhed against him. His silk dress shirt pressed against me.

Why the fuck do I have to be—

I heard it. The lovely, familiar voice of my father. Why the fuck could I hear him? He was talking to someone down on the courtyard patio, almost right beneath us. Why would he bring my dad here? What was he going to do to him?

"Be quiet, and nothing will happen to your father," he whispered.

He eased his hand away, smearing my lipstick further. "If something happens to my father—"

His muscles twitched as he considered covering my mouth again.

"What?" I snapped.

"Your father is here to discuss business, that's all."

"Then why the *fuck* are we up here?"

"Lower your tone, Giovanna." His stern voice crawled along my spine. "We're up here for your punishment."

I cocked my head at him. "What the hell does that even mean?"

Enzo guided me toward the railing overlooking the courtyard. I wanted to ask him what he was doing, but if I could hear the voices below me so clearly, they could certainly hear us. I kept my mouth shut as Enzo put my hands on the railing. I gripped the smooth metal. He got behind me and kicked my legs apart. Anger burned through me until my skin beaded with sweat.

He wouldn't do what he was thinking. He couldn't.

He kissed the back of my neck and leaned close to my ear. "You wanted to come so badly, didn't you, Gia?" he whispered. "So come."

I looked back at him. *I can't,* I mouthed with a shake of my head.

"You will," he breathed against my ear. "I won't stop until you do." His hands trailed down my sides, slowing on every curve of my body. His fingers gripped the bottom of my dress and raised it until the snug fabric bunched at my hips. Cool air hit my ass. It wasn't a cold night, but my body wasn't expecting the sudden loss of coverage.

Enzo liked to play with my head. But this? It was fucking cruel. I couldn't keep quiet, and he knew that. Part of me expected this to be a bluff, that he just wanted to scare me. He didn't scare me, but I got the goddamn point.

He wasn't bluffing as he dropped to his knees, pulled my panties aside, and put his warm tongue on my clit. I fought back a gasp, letting it escape my lips *almost* silently. My father's voice filtered over the rush of my heartbeat in my ears. Enzo licked in long strokes. I squeezed the railing and bit my lip so hard I tasted blood. It took everything in me to keep silent as his tongue raked over me, and I nearly lost it as he did something incredible with his fingers, strumming them against my clit between the strokes of his mouth.

My thighs trembled. I fought everything that was happening. I could hear my father talking, for fuck's sake, and I was supposed to come to that sound?

Fuck you.

I clenched my jaw, trying to focus on that instead of what was happening between my legs.

Enzo climbed from his knees, leaned into me, and placed his wet mouth against my ear. "Stop fighting it," he whispered. "If you don't, I'll fight back."

He slipped down my body and onto his knees again. His tongue went back to work on me, and I clenched my eyes shut, trying to keep the moans hovering in my throat at bay. I leaned into my extended arm, moaning softly into my flesh. I needed to get *something* out or I would end up screaming.

The pleasure built between my legs, but I fought it. I kept my hips stone still instead of bucking against him in hopes of more. I didn't want any more.

Enzo growled behind me. A low, frustrated sound. I was in trouble.

Enzo

Fucking A. She wanted to come so badly a couple nights ago, grinding her sweet pussy against me. Now her rigid posture showed me just how much she was fighting her orgasm. She tried to keep her body calm by letting it course with tension.

I told her if she fought it, I'd fight back.

I pushed two fingers inside her, sinking into her wet warmth in a rushed gesture I hoped would make her cry out. She dropped her head and trembled. Her whole body shook. *You want to come so damn bad, so come.* It wasn't a choice. I would make her come right above her own fucking father.

I climbed off my knees, bracing myself on her perfect ass as I fucked her with my fingers, hard and fast. Wet, excited sounds drifted to my ears, despite her opposition. I fucked her with such force that she spasmed around my fingers. I tugged my hand away, letting her gush onto the concrete, splashing some of her come on the sleeves of my purple dress shirt. I rolled up my sleeve, ready to sink back into her. She trembled and bit her arm, trying to keep herself silent.

I leaned into her ear. "Come from my mouth, and I'll stop. It will all stop."

I reached my hand between her legs and rubbed her, circling her clit from behind with my hard cock pressed against her ass. I got back on my knees and licked her once more, flicking my tongue along her swollen clit. She tasted different once she squirted, but every bit as delicious. My tongue worked her in long, slow strokes as I teased her pussy with my fingers.

She was close. I felt the buildup. She was teetering on her fucking edge. I pushed my fingers inside her, curling them within her as I licked, concentrating on her clit. With her trembling thighs quivering on both sides of my head, she came. She tried to keep her mouth shut, but a long whimper escaped. I stood up and rubbed out the final waves of her orgasm as I clutched my hand around her mouth, and she whimpered against me as I finished her off.

I leaned into her. "I'm not done with you yet, Giovanna."

"Please, no more," she begged as I released her mouth.

I unzipped my pants and pulled out my dick. I was so goddamn hard that it hurt. I'd come so fucking quick in her still-clenching pussy. She didn't have to worry about that. I pushed inside her, covering her mouth again as I forced myself to the depths of her. She spasmed around my cock as I thrust into her.

I fucked her while her father talked to my brother, and knowing my brother was down there made me want to fuck her harder. To keep down the noise from her soaking wet pussy against my pelvis, I settled for grinding against her perfect ass in shallow motions as I thrust inside her. I gripped her hip as I came, filling her pussy until my balls were fucking empty, until I had nothing more to give her.

I pulled out of her, my cock sheening with our come, and tugged down her panties. When she wouldn't step out of them, I took out my knife and cut them off her. I backed away from her, and she shot me a look that could kill. Her makeup was smeared. She was ready to blow up on me.

I smirked and wiped at her mouth, trying to clean the lipstick off her skin. I reached behind the table, grabbed a silk robe, and tried to hand it to her, but she pushed it away.

"You're going to go say hello to your father," I said with a smirk.

Her eyes narrowed. "You just fucking came in me. No."

"That's the point."

"At least let me wear my panties."

"Nope, better keep my come inside you, babygirl. Wouldn't want your daddy to see it dripping down your thighs. Put this on so you don't look so . . ."

"Whore-ish?"

I shrugged. She put on the robe and tied it. When we got in the house, she left her heels inside and walked toward the courtyard patio. She kept her thighs pushed together as she walked, which made me throb. Fuck. It was so goddamn hot. I hoped she could feel my warm come between her legs.

She stepped outside with padded footfalls. My brother looked her up and down.

"Hi, Daddy," she said as she stepped into him and hugged him.

"Gia, how are you?" he asked, his eyes roving over her to see if she was okay. "Are you taking care of her?" Sylvester turned toward me with an accusatory gaze. I didn't even try to hide his daughters come that marked my sleeve as he spoke. "I don't like this arrangement, you know."

"None of us do," Marco chimed in.

I shot him a glare.

"Are you sure you want to be here?" Sylvester turned toward Gia. He made it sound like she wasn't here by choice. She mostly was.

"I'm sure. It's the safest place for me right now," she said firmly. She shifted her weight from one leg to the other, and I imagined my come smearing between her thighs as she tried to keep it from dripping lower. "Well, business," she said with a shrug and backed away, inching toward the door.

I'd let her go clean herself up.

I sat in one of the chairs and stared at her father, who hadn't taken his eyes off me except to look at Gia. He sat across from me.

"Why'd you bring me here, anyway?" he asked me.

"We need to talk about the hit on you. We've been keeping our eyes on the rising bounty, but have you considered fixing whatever the fuck got that put on you? I can't protect you and G—"

"You don't need to protect me, son," Sylvester snapped.

"For her, I do." I gestured inside.

"You're delusional, Viglione, if you think you can be with my daughter."

"Yet here I am, with your daughter."

"You really think you can run your father's business with a rival under your roof? Come on. You know better than that."

He wasn't wrong. It would be a challenge.

"With all due respect, Sylvester, she's old enough to make her own decisions."

"You need to be old enough to make the right ones," Sylvester snapped as he stood up.

I stood and squared off with him. I hated how right he was, but I wasn't willing to admit that yet, not until I knew for sure it couldn't work.

"And don't worry about the hit on me. Stay out of our business. Just because you've made her yours doesn't make Ro and me a part of it. You two are making a mistake, and I thought my daughter was smarter than that."

Sylvester stormed off, tailed by one of his men. I sat down and sighed.

"He's right, you know," Marco said.

"Fuck off," I snapped.

Regardless of who was right or wrong, I wasn't willing to let Gia go until I knew either way.

Chapter Twenty-One

Gia

I sat in my room, seething, with damp hair resting against my shoulders from the shower. I was equal parts pissed and turned on by what happened on the balcony. I liked degradation, but that? That had been something so beyond that. He made me greet my father with his come dripping down my goddamn thighs, claiming me over my own flesh and blood. Any amount of noise beyond my whimpers would have alerted my father to Enzo tonguing the ever-loving fuck out of my pussy. At least when Enzo fucked me, his hand was over my mouth so I could release some muffled frustration against his skin.

Goddamn it, why had I kind of liked it? That pissed me off just as much. I loved and hated being that helpless. Who did Enzo think he was?

As if I'd summoned the demon himself, the door opened. I sat up.

Enzo stared at me as he leaned against the doorframe.

"You mad?" he asked, which made me incredibly fucking mad.

"You have no idea."

He smirked. "I have more of an idea than you think."

My skin flushed hot. "Stop acting like you know so much about me just because you fucked me."

His smirk dropped. He came toward me and grabbed my chin. "I don't think I know so much about you because I've fucked you. I know so much about you because I have watched you from afar for so much longer than you know."

"You . . . stalked me?"

"Consider it more like surveying."

"God, you are disgusting," I said with a humorless laugh.

He leaned over me, releasing my chin to pin my wrists above my head. "The more I degrade you—fuck with you, make you helpless—the more you want me inside you." He kissed me. "So who's the disgusting one?"

"Fuck you." I turned away from his mouth. He was right, though. If he'd allowed it, I'd have let him fill me up again, even though I had just washed his come from my body. Anger flushed my cheeks. But so did something else. "Why did you do that, anyway? You already punished me for what I did. All I did was fucking come." My chest heaved against his.

He looked at me so calmly, so unbothered. It was infuriating. "I fucked your ass because I wanted it. I made you come in front of your father because you didn't. It's real hard to find things you don't want, because you want most everything on some level. I had to find a limit for you." He encased my wrists in one hand, letting the other drop between my legs. "Even then, I don't think that was a limit. You were scared of him hearing his little girl coming. That's a normal fear. Your father shouldn't hear your moans. But I think you wanted my mouth on you and my fingers inside you."

I did. I would always chase the pleasure he offered. I felt alive when he was pleasing me and using me. If I reached the pearly gates and was told I could have Enzo once more or go to heaven, I'd let him fuck me in front of God himself.

"Nothing to say, babygirl? You're only quiet when you're sleeping or brooding. Thinking of ways to get rid of me?"

"You're a piece of shit, but I don't want to get rid of you." How was I so frustrated again? His bright blue eyes met mine, and the way he licked his lips made my mouth water. Through his pants, the hard length of his cock rested against my thigh, and it made me throb. I melted into the mattress and into his grasp. I became the prey beneath him, which would make him become the predator.

"I have work to do. If you want to come to my office later, after everyone goes to bed, I'll be there." He kissed my jaw. "But you know I won't let you come next time we play. You were spoiled." He let go of my wrist and traced my curves with his hand. "But I'll still make you feel good." He dug his fingers into my inner thigh.

I let out a frustrated groan. Everything was a game to Enzo. If I showed any amount of interest, he'd dangle it in front of me, just out of reach. Or pull it away altogether. I never understood why he liked to play the games he did. He denied himself as much as he denied me. How was he not as frustrated? How could he climb off me and leave, just like that? Didn't he ache for me as much?

Enzo

MY BALLS ACHED. I adjusted myself as I swayed in the big overstuffed desk chair. It had been difficult to climb off her when I could feel the heat between her legs against my hard dick. I thumbed through paperwork. So much goddamn paperwork. I was finding out shit I wasn't too fond of. The drug deals, for one thing, with several families on the books for it. I hated that shit. Everyone had a finger in the drug world, even if they didn't dip their whole hand inside. It became something that had to be done to keep afloat in modern crime. Guns and drugs—two big players with big risks.

The clock's *tick-tick-tick* climbed the walls. I felt surrounded by time. I wiped the frustration off my face and pushed the stack of papers away from me. Everything felt so impossible—the business, me leading it. I should have made sure Silvio was more organized before I killed him. Absolutely nothing that was going on surprised me after seeing how our records were kept. I doubted even Silvio knew what was happening with most of this shit.

I groaned and grabbed a cigar, and even though it made me feel like Silvio, I lit it and puffed on it. The rich taste coated my mouth. The scent infiltrated my nose. They were pretty damn magnificent. The smoke swirled and rose toward the high ceiling. The moon cut through the wisps as it shone through the skylight windows. The nicotine took the edge off what made my skin crawl. Stress, anxiety, shit I didn't need to deal with while still trying to pave my way in the business. The unorganized chaos was just a big, shitty cherry on top.

The door to the library slammed. I waved away the thick gray smoke.

Gia. She came. Which I kind of expected. Unfortunately for her, the ache in my balls dissipated the more work frustrated me. I leaned back and puffed on the cigar.

"Hey," she whispered as she walked toward me. Her nose flared as she inhaled the rich scent of the smoke. She perched on the corner of the desk, her shorts riding up her thighs. She twirled her hair as if a million thoughts moved through her mind.

"What's up?" I put my hands behind my head, interlacing them at the fingers.

"You told me to meet you here."

"I know I did, but I'm not really in the mood anymore. I spent hours going through paperwork, and I hardly made a dent in it. I found out Silvio was involved in some drug dealings, which—"

"You hate," she interrupted. That was no secret. "But everyone has to get their hands a little dirty with that stuff. Even my father has a couple contacts in that business."

"The golden boy?"

"Yes, even the golden boy." She smirked. "Are we going to finish off what we started earlier?"

I wanted to. I really wanted to. But I also just wanted to burn this library to the ground with all the paperwork inside it. "Babygirl," I said, low and smooth.

"Don't babygirl me unless you're going to do something about it." She got to her feet, dropped her elbows to the desk, and thumbed through the stack of papers. My eyes traced every curve of her body as she bent over the way I'd fantasized a thousand times in my head. She pulled several papers from the pile and leaned over me to grab a thick fastener folder filled with hole-punched paper. She skimmed through the pages and whipped it open, laying it out in front of me. "These are all collected and can be tossed, burned, whatever the hell you want to do with them."

"How do you know?" I leaned over the desk, pulling my attention from her.

"Our fathers aren't all that different, Enzo. See these little symbols and numbers on the corners of these debt slips?" Her finger dragged down the paper in front of me. "They match up in the log here. Instead of using the debtors' names, he uses the numbers and symbols to mark off when someone paid. This little triangle matches this little triangle in that folder. Forty-five thousand, paid off in September almost five years ago. That's why he kept these debt slips, so he knew who borrowed what without a clear link of what happened. What I can't tell you is where Silvio put said money, as he didn't seem to write that on either document. So I can't help you there."

I grabbed the slips, checking them against the log. I flashed my eyes up at her. "All this fucking time I've spent trying to figure out the method to his madness, and you figure it out in five minutes."

"You never let me look at them like this. Sometimes you just need an outsider's perspective."

When she said the word outsider, my stomach tightened. That was exactly what I was doing, letting an outsider gain perspective on my family business. It was so fucking stupid. I needed to protect our inside information, but I wanted to let Gia in so damn bad. She tilted her head with condescending pride. What made her so trustworthy? How could I expose our underbelly to her and hope she wouldn't rip it open? She represented generations of our enemies.

Gia wasn't my enemy, but should she have been?

I stood up, and when she went to stand beside me, I fisted her hair and held her down, leaning over her as I tightened my grasp. I craned her neck and forced her to look at me. "I don't think I need to tell you how fucking dumb this is. You could destroy us. You could leave here and destroy *me*. You will learn things that you'd have to take to your grave, and I'm not sure you can. You have a big mouth, Giovanna, and an even bigger taste for revenge. All it would take is for you to get mad at me, like you always do."

Her lips parted and she let out a whimper as she strained against my painful hold of her hair. Her dark eyes met mine. "My father is an unofficial informant to someone in the FBI."

I cocked my head at her and tugged her up, still craning her neck. "What the fuck do you mean?"

"He grew up with someone in the FBI. He feeds them little bits of information to keep them off our backs."

"And you're telling me this now? After I let you into my—"

"Your family isn't on our radar. Not like that. My father is more interested in taking out the legs of smaller families."

"You don't infiltrate people who aren't on your radar."

"My father was considering an alliance."

"Why should I fucking trust you or your rat of a father?"

"Because you have something over me now. Over my family. If I betray you, the means are there to get me and my family killed."

She was right . . . if she was telling the truth. Her steady lower lip made me think she was. But knowing her father was an informant, even unofficially, made it all seem so much more of a risk than what it was worth. Yeah, I could get her family killed over that, but it would require commands from federal fucking prison.

Was she worth that risk?

Chapter Twenty-Two

Gia

I most definitely did not get laid after admitting my father's informal informant status. Enzo sent me away, and deservedly so. He had a lot to think about. I did too, because I had placed something that could destroy me and my family into his hands. His family was notoriously impulsive, and I just handed the biggest Silvani secret to him on a silver fucking platter. He could pretend to understand my taste for revenge all he wanted, but he was bloodthirsty for it, too. Reckless. If he decided to reject me, cast me out of his life, would he hold that secret for me or let me burn? I felt as though I were waiting to learn my sentence from a jury of my peers. Maybe it was the executioner. Either way, I didn't like the uncertainty.

There was a knock on the door. I assumed it would be Enzo, but it was one of his men. "Enzo would like to see you in his room," the man said, much too prim and proper.

It had been hours since he banished me from the library, and I assumed he went back to his room to sleep off his frustrations. I'd hoped he'd woken up with a clearer head. Maybe a clearer heart.

With silent footsteps, I walked barefoot toward his room, and I entered after a quick knock. Atheist leaped off the bed and ran toward me. He sat at my feet, his big pink tongue lolling out of his mouth as he panted with excitement. I rubbed the velvet fur on his blocky head, talking high and sweet to him, which just made him wag his body harder.

Enzo came out of the bathroom. He was still wearing his slacks, though his belt was unbuckled. His revolver rested on his hip, unshielded by his sleeveless ribbed t-shirt. He looked torn up, mentally and physically. He dropped onto the couch, not even taking the time to pull his belt from the loops. Both ends flopped loosely on his lap. He drew a cigarette and lit it, and I watched his mouth as he inhaled and exhaled, wishing he'd use it to say something to me.

He exhaled a thick wave of smoke. "I finally have you back, and I feel compelled—pressured—to push you away again."

My heart sank to somewhere beneath my stomach. My insides felt rearranged, and not in a good way. How was I supposed to offer a rebuttal? Beg him? I didn't have it in me. I had to understand, even if I didn't want to, that it was all for the betterment of the business. It had nothing to do with *me* or *us*.

"I know," I said.

He looked straight ahead as he smoked. "I don't want to rot in prison and throw away everything I've worked for."

"I know."

"But I don't want to be without you, either." He finally met my gaze. His eyes looked sad and torn. "Let's get married," he said with a final puff of the cigarette before squelching it out on the tray.

My mouth dropped open and stayed that way. I couldn't reel in my expression. *Did he just say we should get married? Fucking married? Like . . . real life marriage?* "I—"

"You ain't gotta look at me like that, Gia." He wiped his chin. "A no would suffice."

"No . . . I mean . . . no, I'm not saying no," I stammered. "But I don't know if I'm saying yes. I don't want to get married just to show you that you can trust me."

"That's not why I want to get married. I want to get married because you're mine. There ain't a way for people to push you out when you are that in, Giovanna. You'd be a Viglione. If you took me down, you'd be going for the ride with me."

"Again, it sounds like you want to marry me to protect your business," I snapped.

He motioned me over to him without saying a word. On a normal day, I'd tell him to fuck off for gesturing to me like I was a dog. But today, with so much looming over us, I walked past Atheist and sat on his lap. The clasp of his belt dug into my bare thigh. He kissed me hard on the mouth, and his hand ran down my neck with a tenderness I didn't expect.

"I want to marry you to make you a part of my business. You'd be mine. *Truly* mine. You wouldn't belong to your father anymore. You'd belong to *me*."

I kissed him back, forgetting about everything but his lips and the way they moved against mine. The world could be on fire, burning around us, scalding our skin, and I wouldn't feel a damn thing except his hand on my neck. That was why I loved Enzo. When it seemed like life couldn't get any more cold or black, he raised me until the sun warmed my skin and lit up everything around me. I knew I would fight it—and fight him—but I took each breath for him. For this.

I sat in silence, soaking him in, my forehead against his. I met his gaze. "If you can get my father's blessing, I'll marry you."

Enzo cocked his eyebrow as he pulled away from me. "You really don't want to get married, do you?"

I smirked. "No, I do. I just can't without my father's approval, and you know that."

"You could," he corrected.

"I can't," I said, more firmly.

"He ain't ever gonna let me marry you, Giovanna. He hates me. You and I may not be enemies, but me and him are. He doesn't want you with me, so how the hell do you expect me to convince him to let me *marry* you?"

"You're resourceful. If you want it bad enough, you'll figure it out."

Enzo fisted my hair and kissed me with a frustrated groan. "Fine, plan on it, babygirl, because I won't stop until I can make you a Viglione."

I knew that. I knew he would stop at nothing to make me his, to keep me. His touch sent a shiver from the tips of his fingers wrapped in my hair to the base of my spine, where his other hand rested.

"Come with me," he growled.

"Where?"

"To the library." He stepped toward the door, but spun on his heels and tugged my arm. "Now, Giovanna," he commanded.

"But—" I didn't want to go into the library. I wanted him to fuck me right where we were, away from prying eyes and needless questions.

"Now!" His blue eyes deepened into the intoxicating shade that made me drunk.

I followed him as if in a trance. The muscles in his back flexed beneath the thin fabric of his sleeveless shirt. He didn't even bother to buckle his belt in his haste, and it clanged together with every step. I looked around with a nervousness I didn't like feeling. I was waiting for Marco to come around the corner. Maybe Sammy. Enzo pushed the library door open, dragged me inside, and guided me toward his desk.

Everything was so much different from the first time I walked into this library—my feet were bare now, there were no armed guards, and Enzo was at the helm instead of Silvio. When Enzo sat at the big desk and dropped his head back with a contented sigh, I slipped into my mind, still remembering that day. Silvio's fat cheeks, gone, replaced by Enzo's perfect features. Silvio's bad attitude, gone . . . mostly. Our lives? Totally different now. Enzo hated me then, and sometimes he still did, but what sat behind that desk now was someone who loved to love me, even when he didn't want to. I wanted to help him become the leader he dreamed of becoming, the figurehead his father never could be. I wished I could make him believe that.

"Come cross-check some more of these debt slips," Enzo whispered.

"What? Now? It's, like, four in the morning."

"Can you ever just do what I ask?" He wiped his chin, leaving his hand to hover over it. He looked strong. Powerful. And it made me want to be fucking weak.

I rolled my eyes and dropped my elbows to the desk like I had earlier. I picked up several slips, a pen, and went to work. A quick motion of the pen was all it took to mark the ones that were paid. I picked up the next one, but before I could drop my eyes to the logbook, Enzo's hand crept up my thigh with an electric touch. I tried to focus on the symbols and numbers, but he shoved his knee between my legs, spreading my thighs in a rough motion and distracting me. His hands were on me. One moved down the curve of my spine as the other tugged my shorts aside and rubbed between my legs. I tried to control the desperate whimpers. I wanted him so damn bad.

I had dreamed of this exact moment, bent over Silvio's— well, Enzo's—desk. I had never wanted anything more, but I had to keep myself in control. If he knew how badly I wanted it, he'd withhold all of it. I'd get nothing.

"Don't stop working," he commanded as he hooked his hands into my waistband and pulled down my shorts. I let them fall to the floor and kicked them away, and his hand grazed my ass.

"Yes, sir," I said with a mocking salute. Playing it cool was clearly not my strong suit.

He groaned. "I kind of liked you calling me sir."

"Don't expect it," I said as I marked another debt slip. "Sir."

"Fuck, Giovanna, I have made myself come so many times to what I'm looking at right now. You, bent over my desk with your perfect ass up in the air. So goddamn wet," he growled as he rubbed his fingers between my legs. "You'd think fantasy would look better than reality, but no. You are fucking perfection."

I shivered at his words. He unholstered his revolver and set it on the table beside me, and my eyes locked on the piece of metal. I bit my lip.

"What is it with you and that goddamn gun?" he asked as he put his hand over it again. All six brassy bullets gleamed in the chambers. "Keep working," he commanded as he lifted the gun and ran the cold barrel between my shoulder blades. My nerves awakened beneath the thin fabric of my cami. I didn't care that his gun was loaded. It only heightened my excitement.

Enzo put pressure into the barrel against my spine as he drove it downward. I trusted him with my life. He'd keep me safe, even as his breaths grew ragged. The tip of the barrel was warm by the time it reached my ass, but it made me jolt with a chill as he put it against my pussy.

"Don't jump like that, babygirl. Not when I have a loaded gun on you," he said as he leaned his weight into me, pushing me into the front of the desk.

I dropped my head as he rubbed the gun, back and forth, over my swollen clit. I was painfully turned on, struggling to keep my composure.

"Do you know how many men I've killed with this gun? Do you wanna guess?"

I marked off another slip. I had no fucking clue how many people Enzo had killed. Probably a fucking lot. "Five," I blurted. So much for keeping my composure.

"Close . . ." he whispered. He angled the gun to keep the front sight off my clit, but he turned it a bit wrong every so often, and it would rake my clit just enough for ripples of pain to vibrate through me. I bit my lip as he did it again. "I've killed eight men with this gun. Or is it nine?" He stopped the motion for a moment as he thought. "Either way, men have died staring down this barrel, and you're trying to come from it. What the hell is wrong with you, Giovanna?"

There we go again—a fucking lot. Was that an answer? A lot was wrong with me.

I kept trying to do what he said, to work and keep my

focus on the slips in front of me, but I tilted my pelvis, grinding on the barrel of his revolver until it became slick with my wetness. I expected him to stop me and put a halt to everything, but he kept going. I kept moving my hips against his gun. Pleasure burned through me and the source of the fire was the heat between my legs. Enzo groaned. He knew by the way I breathed and tensed that I was close. My stomach tightened, fearing he'd stop me right at my point of no return. I wanted to come while grinding on his gun.

"Don't stop working," he whispered as he wrapped his free hand around me, ran it up my shirt, and gripped my chest. His fingertips dug into my breast.

My writing became nothing more than a blip on paper as he pushed me over the edge and let me fall. I came hard, shuddering against the desk, the pen in a death grip as my entire body tensed and tightened. His hand moved between my breasts and wrapped around my throat, squeezing the sides of my neck. The dizzying pleasure washed over me as I rode out the final waves of my orgasm against the warm, slick metal.

He pulled the gun away, and I felt vacant without it between my legs. He aimed it at the ceiling, and my come dripped down the barrel.

"Lick your come off my gun, babygirl. You know I love watching your tongue on the metal as you clean up your mess for me. It's almost as good as watching your mouth on my dick."

He put it to my lips, and I looked up at him as I wrapped my hands around his wrist and licked up the barrel. The sweet metallic taste hit my tongue, and I moaned as I cleaned it off for him. He growled and stared at my tongue curving around the barrel.

"It's not enough. Get on your knees," he commanded, his gun still in his hand.

"What do you want?" I asked as I eyed his body.

He undid his pants, pulled out his cock, and rested the butt of his revolver on his thigh so the barrel was beside his dick. "Lick both," he said as he gave himself a quick stroke.

I looked up at him as I licked the underside of his dick, then did the same with the cool metal barrel. As I tasted both him and the extension of him, he let out a groan. When I focused on his gun, my hand stroked his dick.

"You're such a good girl," he whispered as he dropped his head back.

I took the barrel and his cock and pressed them side by side, then licked them at the same time. The contrasting tastes of metal and his body wash fought in my mouth.

He put his revolver on the desk and fisted my hair, putting himself in my mouth for a few rough thrusts. He growled and pulled me to my feet, looking at me as if he were starving for me. Beyond starving. As if he'd die right then if he didn't push himself inside what belonged to him.

"Remember what I said to you?" he asked as he put me on the edge of his desk.

"Which time?"

"When we woke up a few days ago," he said. "I told you I'd make you come . . . and then I'd make you come with me inside your ass."

My mind swam. I *really* didn't think he'd let me come twice, but I was also really uncomfortable with the idea of him fucking me that way again.

A bead of excitement gathered and dripped down the swollen head of his cock. He rubbed his dick along my pussy. When he grazed my clit, it made me jolt. He coated himself with my come.

"Enzo," I whispered as he pressed the head of his cock against me. I must have looked weak and scared, because he let his tough demeanor falter for a moment. He grabbed my face, brushing my dark hair away from it. He kissed me.

"Let me make you feel good," he whispered against my mouth. "I ain't them." He meant the men who took me against my will.

I took a deep breath and leaned back onto my hands. I spread my legs wider for him. I trusted him with so much of me. Why not that, too?

He groaned as he leaned back and spit between my legs. The warmth slid over my pussy and spread around his dick. He rubbed it on himself before gripping his cock. I sucked in a breath as he inched into me. I bit my lip as I fought a reaction from the pain. He was so careful and slow as he buried himself inside me.

He closed the distance between us and pushed his fingers inside me. I gasped at how full he made me feel. His thumb circled my swollen clit. He touched me better than I could touch myself. With each slow, patient thrust, I felt everything to my very core.

"You feel so good, Giovanna," he growled as he kissed me. "I want you to come with me deep inside you."

With the way his hips curled into mine and how his fingers played me, I quit worrying he'd stop. He was trying too hard to please me. Or at least that's what I tried to tell myself.

The pain from his cock lessened until it was mostly pleasurable. His fingers curled within me. His thumb rubbed me. Hell was where I thought I belonged, but right then, with pleasure coursing through every fiber of my being, I was in fucking heaven. I stopped controlling my moans and relaxed deeper, letting the pleasure wash over me. Like a goddamn tidal wave, it pulled me under the water, where I'd become one with the sea.

I shuddered with a full body orgasm that made me question if I was in some sort of dream or fantasyland instead of real life, and I made him come as he chased my pleasure. It was no dream. No fantasy. He was my perfect reality.

Chapter Twenty-Three

Enzo

I woke up beside Gia. It felt eerily similar to the last time I woke up beside her, except this time, I didn't think she'd be upset about what I'd done to her. I had thoroughly used her up, and I loved every second of it. I knew she had, too.

I tugged my arm from under her, and she whined. We had slept late, which was my fault. By the time I was done with her and we showered away all our come, it was nearly six in the morning.

I stepped into a pair of sweatpants and sat on the couch. I had to think about my game plan regarding the O'Rileys, because I'd been ignoring it. With Gia asleep, and having given into her as much as I had, I could focus. Probably.

Atheist leaped off the floor and greeted me with a full-body wiggle. "If it ain't her, it's you," I said as I gripped his ears in my hands. "Do I have to get rid of both of ya?" I rubbed the top of his head. Atheist was supposed to be a guard dog. I had intended to raise a monster. I failed.

Hard. He was protective, and so damn loyal, but mean? Nah. Not a mean bone in all one hundred and fifteen pounds of him. He didn't need to be, though. When people saw him, he looked mean, and that's what mattered. Instead of raising him like an employee, I raised him as my best friend. Sometimes, the only one I had. I wouldn't take a bullet for that damn dog, but I'd do just about anything else for him. Gia, though? I'd take several for her. I had no intention of getting rid of either of them, even if they both distracted me from my job. "Do you gotta go out?" I asked. He jumped down and ran for the door.

The sun was high in the sky, and its heat warmed my back through my shirt. I was surprised he waited so long to wake me up. He trotted across the lawn when I opened the gate, and I smoked a cigarette as I waited for him to do his business. My eyes caught a glimpse of motion. Something caught Atheist's as well. His body rumbled with a growl, and his muscles tensed. I just got through thinking how he was a pitiful guard dog, but something was pissing him off.

The movement belonged to my brother Marco. He leaned against the front of the building as he chatted with another man and brushed a hand through his hair, a nervous habit we both had. I couldn't tell what they were saying with the glare from the sun behind them, but I knew my brother, and his posture told me he was uncomfortable. I put the cigarette between my lips and tried to listen, but they hushed their words.

Who the hell is that? I didn't recognize the man. He had blond, brushed-back hair, and he wore a dress shirt with the cuffs of his sleeves folded over. He had to have been our age. Why the hell would Marco host a meeting without me? Granted, I slept much too late, and they all knew not to bother me when I was asleep unless someone was dead or dying.

I leaned against the metal pole behind me and watched. Neither had noticed me, even over the loud squeal of the gate as it opened and closed. I turned back toward Atheist, who remained planted where he stood. The sun glinted against his jet-black coat. I didn't like how he looked at them.

There was a shift in the air, a heaviness that lowered on both of us. My fingers wrapped around the gate as I pulled it open. The yard past the gate and fencing around the house was open because Atheist never went far, and it kept the shit and piss away from the patio area. Before I could recall him, he bounded across the yard toward the two men. It wasn't his playful run. It was a hard, dedicated stride that made me cock my head. I'd only seen him do that a handful of times, but he'd return when I recalled, stopping in his tracks at the sound of my voice. I called his name, but his paws continued pounding the earth as he charged toward them.

I quickened my steps when I heard a scream accompanied by aggressive snarling. Marco yelled Atheist's name. By the time I made it over to them, Atheist had latched on. The man's entire forearm was in the wide, gnashing jaws of my dog as he swung his body, trying to fend him off. Atheist snarled as he bit harder and shook. His massive head jerked side to side as he bit to maim, focused on ripping the man's arm clean off.

"Fuck!" the man screamed, spit exploding from his mouth as he yelled. He leaned back on his heels, trying to keep on his feet. If he went down, Atheist would go for his throat.

Everything happened in seconds, but it felt like so much

longer. The man panted through screams as Marco tried to get between them. Every time he tried, my dog just bit harder. Marco snatched at Atheist's collar as the man screamed out again, trying to rip his arm out of my dog's mouth. The more he tried to pull away, the more Atheist dug his heels in. I called out to Atheist as blood dripped down the man's forearm and puddled on the concrete. The crimson stained his nice dress shirt and spread upward with every passing second.

The man drew his gun and raised it. Everything slowed down as the pistol's silver inched toward Atheist. I could see nothing but the gun and my dog, the single most important thing in my entire life aside from Gia. I heard the thump of every beat of my heart, drowning out the screams.

"If you shoot my dog, I will fucking kill you and everything you have ever loved!" I screamed over the thunder of my heart in my ears. I would. If he put down my dog, he'd be next. I didn't have my revolver, which was fucking stupid, but if I had to use my pocketknife to rip him open from mouth to asshole, I would.

The man met my gaze, his face contorted in pain. The green of his irises swirled in his bloodshot eyes. He looked familiar, but I couldn't place it. He kept his gun aimed at my dog but moved his finger off the trigger.

I pushed Marco aside and grabbed Atheist's collar. He had pulled the man down until he'd gotten all four paws on the ground, yanking the mangled flesh like he was in a game of tug-of-war. I had never seen that dog do that. It was like he was a different animal, not the one I raised.

"Get your goddamn dog off me!" the man screeched. Blood poured in thick red lines over his pale skin and dripped down his slacks, even staining his sock. It was a damn mess.

I lifted Atheist by the collar, his front paws dangling. The man yelled out. I twisted the leather, which did jack shit around his meaty neck. He refused to let go.

When the man's finger wrapped around the trigger again, I socked Atheist in the mouth in a last-ditch effort to get him to release. I didn't want to punch him, but a quick jab was better than the bullet. His blood-soaked muzzle released, and he looked at me with as much confusion as I had about him. His eyes, which were always so soft and round, were hard and focused. If I let go of his collar, he'd be on that man again in an instant. I had never seen such a thing. Atheist didn't hate anyone like that, especially someone we'd never met.

"He ain't ever acted like that," I said as I held back a dog that very much looked like he acted like that. Atheist let out a rumbling bark from the depths of his belly. Blood dripped from his jowls. He looked like fucking Cujo.

The man sneered, grabbing his arm and cradling it with his other. Atheist's body vibrated as he growled. Marco was just frozen in confusion. Neither of us would have expected that from my dog. No one spoke as I backed away, tugging him with me. He dug his heels in, trying to turn his head and body back toward the man like I was leading him away from a steak fucking dinner. I had to get him upstairs. I'd hear about it later, and deservedly so, but all I cared about was getting him away from whoever the fuck *that* was.

I slammed the door behind me, startling Gia, who was just getting out of bed. Even though Atheist was acting like what happened back there never happened, I didn't let go of his collar. Gia tensed when she saw the look on my face, and she made a move to stand up when she saw his blood-stained fur.

"What the hell happened?" she asked.

"I have no fucking clue. He just attacked some guy my brother was having a meeting with. I mean, *attacked*. I had to punch him to get him off the guy so he didn't get shot. I ain't ever seen him like that." My words erupted out of me, still half in disbelief.

It was hard to imagine the dog beside me, now wagging his tail and body as if nothing happened, had done what he did. As if there wasn't blood staining his damn mouth.

"You know what they say about dogs." Gia got out of bed and patted Atheist's head. "They know more than we do about a person."

She came over and kissed me, which was enough to calm my ailing nerves. I'd seen a lot of horrible shit that would keep any sane person up at night, but that? Watching my boy turn into something I couldn't control, something hell-bent on killing a person, that was worse than anything I'd ever seen.

"This dog has only ever bitten Silvio," I said with a shake of my head.

Oh.

I smirked at Atheist. I was certain if that was the case, he bit Silvio because he was a shit person. So what the hell kind of person was the man he just mauled out there in front of our house?

Chapter Twenty-Four

Gia

I walked into the kitchen. The waiter popped out from the door on the other side of the room, scaring the shit out of me.

"Can I get you something, ma'am?" he asked.

"No, I'm fine. Thank you, though," I said. "Also, you can call me Gia."

He smiled politely, and I knew he wouldn't call me by my name. He brushed long black hair from his face and disappeared into the back room.

I grabbed a wine glass hanging above the island counter and poured some wine, taking a hearty swig before I even put the cap back on. Enzo had gotten his ass chewed out last night by Marco, but he was being weird about the strange man. We still had little idea about who he was or why Marco had met with him. I had never heard Enzo yell like that. But he was defending the honor of his dog and his home. In the end, they parted ways because neither would get anything out of the other while emotions were running so high. Marco demanded that Enzo get his outfit dry cleaned. I had doubts that the amount of blood would come out.

Enzo stormed out after their fight, leaving me alone with the beast himself. Atheist was nothing but the lovable lug he'd always been. I wouldn't have believed what Enzo had told me if I hadn't seen the blood on Atheist's mouth with my own eyes. Or the video, when Enzo pulled up the camera. I would have thought that was a vicious black bear, not the dog I slept with whenever I was in there with Enzo. It was horrifying. I'd only seen men that hell-bent on killing. What the fuck had him so freaked out? None of us recognized the man. Clearly, Atheist recognized *something* in him that we couldn't see.

My phone buzzed. I looked at it as I inhaled more of my drink. A text from Enzo. I hadn't heard from him since he ran off this morning, doing god knows what. Whatever it was, I wasn't invited.

Meet me in my room.

I refilled my glass before capping off and putting the wine back in the fridge. I made my way to Enzo's side of the house. I opened his door, pushing Atheist aside as I walked in. Empty. Where the hell was he?

Heavy steps sounded outside. I saw his shadow on the balcony and unlocked the door and let him in. His breaths were still heavy. His eyes were deep and dark. *What the hell did he get into?* When he stepped into the light, I saw the blood. He had taken off his dress shirt before whatever he'd done, but blood splattered across his undershirt and crimson marked his skin. It had dried over the array of ink across his shoulders and chest.

"Wh-what the hell happened to you?" I stammered.

"Ensuring you'd be my goddamn wife." He removed his shirt and tossed it in the garbage. I stared at his taut abdomen, muscles rippling with the same frustration broadcast from every step he took.

I was lost. I had no fucking clue what he was talking about. I could hardly keep myself together as I watched him step closer. He reached toward me with a hand still covered in dry blood and wrapped it around the back of my neck. I put my hands between us and kept him at arm's length. I liked to pretend I had any control if Enzo decided to close the gap.

"I'm going to need you to stop and explain," I said, growing annoyed with his ambiguity. "Whose blood is all over you?"

"Ugo Moretti."

I cocked my head. "Am I supposed to know that name?"

"Your father does."

"For fuck's sake, Enzo, what the hell are you talking about?"

He was riding the high of a good murder. And it annoyed me.

"Ugo put the hit out on your father, and it died with him."

I shook my head. "Wait, what? You killed the man who put the hit on my father? Wh—how—"

"I found out who was behind it all, which was a pain in the ass," Enzo seethed through a tense jaw. "But for how well he protected his identity, he didn't protect himself enough."

"Did he say why?"

"He said Sylvester got their chain of underground casinos shut down. I don't know if that was the real reason, but under duress, it's all he had to say."

"Did you torture him?"

"Abso-fucking-lutely."

"And you didn't bring me?"

Enzo shook his head. "Too dangerous. I needed to be a Viglione to do what I had to do, and it's real hard to be a true Viglione with you around. I'd hate for you to see the raw me. It would be as shocking to you as it was for me to see Atheist act so against his nature. Except that what I just did is exactly *my* nature. You see glimpses of it every so often, but you've never seen me unleashed. I'd like to keep it that way."

I couldn't believe what I was hearing. The bounty? Gone. Just like that. My father was safe—for now—and Enzo was a hero. Though no one else would see it that way. The Morettis—I realized who they were only after Enzo mentioned the casinos—absolutely had a reason to want my father dead. He got their entire chain shut down so he could run his casinos nearly unrivaled. Was it a dick move? Yeah. But it wasn't personal. It was business.

"If we get married, I'd probably see that side of you."

"That's true," he whispered, leaning closer to me. "But I'd have no reason to hide it from you any longer."

There was thick silence between us. "Did he suffer?" I finally asked, unable to hide the excitement in my voice.

"God, you are such a Cosa Nostra. I bet you're wet from it, huh?" His hand rose up my leggings and landed on my thighs. "Do you wanna know what I did?" he asked.

I nodded with a bite of my lip.

"Take off your pants, babygirl," he commanded.

I had them halfway down my thighs before he even finished his sentence. I slipped them down and kicked them off.

Enzo rubbed his fingers along my red panties. "I broke

into his home." He kissed me. "I made him tell me what I wanted to know by cutting off his fingers, one by one. And when that didn't work, I cut off his ears. He wasn't fucking listening anyway." He bit my lip as he pulled away from me. "Do you wanna know what I did to him once he told me what issue he had with your father?" Enzo stared at me as he pushed my panties aside and backed me against the dresser. He undid his slacks, tugging out his cock. He was so damn hard. That's what was fucked up about the whole thing, how damn excited we were.

"Tell me, Enzo." I panted the words.

He lifted one of my legs and pushed his cock inside me. I gasped as he pinned me against the dresser with each thrust. The cold wood nipped at the backs of my bare thighs. I wrapped my arms around his neck, and my fingers traced his tattoos and the blood that coated them.

"I couldn't shoot him. Too loud. So I slit his throat, which is when most of this blood splatter happened." He thrust each word into me so I could ride the same high. "Will you fucking marry me yet?" he growled into my neck. The metallic scent of death surrounded him.

"You have to talk to my father," I said through a moan.

"Goddamn it, Giovanna," he groaned, his breath rolling over my neck. "What do I have to do to make you my wife? What more do I have to do? I've taken every piece of you, every part of your body. I've given you parts of me in return that I've never given to another person." He lifted his head and ran his bloody fingers up my chest, grazing my neck before he wrapped his hand around my throat. He squeezed the sides of my neck, letting the pleasure wash over me.

I needed my father's approval. He knew that. I would be turning away from my family completely if I didn't have it. I couldn't do that, no matter how much I wanted to.

Enzo's eyes narrowed on me. "What if I told you I wouldn't fuck you again until you agree to be my wife?" His words pissed me off, no matter how low and sensual they were. I didn't respond. My cheeks flamed red. "Is that what you want, Giovanna? Because I'll pull out of your perfect pussy right now."

"Fuck you."

Enzo tightened the grip on my throat, spreading my legs wider with a rough grasp. "No, fuck *you*," he snarled back, thrusting so hard that I had to grip his shoulders. He pulled out of me, turned me around, and pushed my chest onto the dresser. He pushed himself back inside me. "Enjoy this, babygirl. Not *too* much, though, because after I fill you up, it will be the last until you decide to stop being such a *Silvani*." He said my last name with disgust, and it made me fucking weak. "I really don't know why I bother trying. You aren't even worth it." He knew exactly what to say to break me in all the right ways. "This pussy is worth it, but you? It ain't worth the trouble."

"I'm not worth it, Enzo." I moaned out the words as he craned my neck. His free hand wrapped around me and grabbed my breasts through my cami. With a frustrated groan, he ripped the fabric so he could get his selfish, hungry touch on my bare skin.

"Don't you even think of coming," he snarled. "I won't let you come until you decide whether you want to be my wife or remain a Silvani. After you make your choice, whatever you choose, then I'm going to make you come. Either you'll agree to be my wife, or I'll fuck you so good that once you leave here, you'll never be the same. You won't ever be a true Silvani again. Mark my words, Giovanna. You will always be mine, and I want you to remember that if you decide to stay a Silvani. You'll think of me every time you fuck another man."

He growled and finished inside me, filling me exactly as he promised while leaving me wanting more. I'd make my decision . . . after he talked to my father.

Chapter Twenty-Five

Enzo

Intrusive thoughts rattled around in my head as I tried to focus on the task at hand: doing business with one of Silvio's old clients. I could only think of Gia. That was the problem with driving alone. I could only interact with my own mind. I wasn't kidding when I told her I'd stop having sex with her. I would withhold what she wanted most until she made a decision. I'd done horrible things for her, and all I wanted in return was . . . well, her. All of her.

I shouldn't have killed Ugo, and I probably hadn't needed to torture him, either. It didn't really matter *why* he put the hit out on Gia's father, but I knew she'd ask. She'd *need* to know, and I wanted to be able to tell her. I could have guessed—a large chunk of her father's business revolved around gambling, and it wasn't out of the realm of possibility that he'd take down his competitor—but was it really worth that bounty on his head? I wasn't sure. I also didn't know how her father would react to the news that I'd gotten rid of the hit for him. For Gia, actually. Would that be enough for him to give me his blessing to marry her? Sylvester was a wildcard. Even so, I had to tell him I'd saved his ass before someone else could take credit for my work.

Something else made me nervous about that, though. Once I told him who I killed and why, there would be little to keep him quiet about it. He could take me down with what I'd done to protect him. He could use that to destroy me and protect his daughter. But I had to try. I couldn't *not* try. I'd never wanted anything more in my life than to make Gia a Viglione. I wanted it even more than my desire to become a don. Now it felt like one couldn't happen without the other, and I wasn't willing to let go of either.

I'd get it over with and talk to Sylvester after I finished the little transaction with one of the usuals. There were certain clients who would only do business with Silvio. Now they'd only do business with me.

My phone chimed and I looked at the message. It was from Bullseye's sister, checking in on my search for information. Which wasn't happening. I knew all I needed to know, and they were all things I couldn't let her find out. I sighed and put down the phone.

The sun edged across the horizon as I pulled into the familiar parking lot. Something felt off. Different. I parked and looked around as I got out of the car. There was nothing out of the ordinary, even if it felt like it. Cars dotted the lot the same way they always had. I started toward the door of the swanky dance club set back from the road. I had to get going if I wanted to talk to Sylvester before the old man went to sleep at fucking eight o'clock. I wiped a hand through my hair and told myself to stop being so paranoid.

Nothing was out of the ordinary . . . aside from the metal barrel prodding my back.

"Hands up," the voice said behind me, calm and cool.

I had no intention of putting my hands up. I didn't show weakness. If I ended up dead, it'd be with my goddamn dignity intact. "Fuck off," I said through clenched teeth. "Who are you?" I had ideas—it could have been so many people—but I didn't recognize the voice.

A gloved hand reached out and disarmed me, taking my beloved revolver off my hip. "You'll find out."

Footfalls landed behind me. It sounded like it was just the two of them. If they put the guns down and fought fair, I was pretty certain I could take them.

"Pussies," I snarled.

They placed a dark hood over my head. I would have fought, but the barrel was still pressed into me, reminding me that I was in an unwinnable situation. They bound my wrists in front of me with tape and pushed me into the back-seat of a car. The men got in, and the car lurched forward. Road noise rumbled louder and clearer with my sense of sight gone.

I was fucking pissed. The longer we were in the car, the more I seethed, but I had to keep my composure. I was a don. I couldn't let myself seem weak. But how could I fight? Even before they disarmed me, it was a pistol against a goddamn rifle, and he already had one up on me.

"You'll regret this," I told them. They'd have no choice but to kill me, because if I got a fraction of a chance, I'd kill them.

I LOOKED around an unfamiliar basement as they removed the hood. Tools and machinery cluttered the space, but nothing gave any indication of who had taken me, and they didn't seem inclined to tell me why.

Ransom? Marco would let them keep me.

Retribution? That hardly eliminated anyone from the list of suspects.

Yeah, those were pretty much the two options. I'd pissed someone off. But I'd pissed off a lot of people over the years.

Blood stains painted the floor. They'd been cleaned up, of course, but blood didn't come out of concrete like this. That's why we started covering the floor with plastic drop cloths. It took some of the cleanup out of our crimes. Also, the moment someone walked into a plastic-clad room, they knew their blood would be shed. It made them more willing to talk. Mental warfare.

A man wearing cargo pants and a dark, long-sleeved shirt greeted me. A mask obscured his face, so I had no fucking clue who he was. I assumed it had something to do with the O'Rileys. I never took the time to figure that situation out because I'd been too busy fucking around with Gia. If it was the O'Rileys, I had no one to blame but myself. I'd executed Bullseye, and it had been my idea to bring the car to Jameson. When Gia had offered to sleep with him for his silence, I couldn't handle it, and I killed the Irish prick. I'd been too preoccupied with Gia to deal with the aftermath of such a stupid political move.

Yeah, if it was the O'Rileys, I deserved to be in this situation.

"Be a man and show your face," I said.

"In good time, Mr. Viglione. Once you see my face, you'll know your time is nearly up."

"Killing me is probably a wise choice," I snapped. I sank back against the wall and kicked my feet out with a heavy sigh. It wouldn't solve a damn thing if I panicked. As Gia would say, such is this life. When our victims panicked and begged, it was that much more delicious. You almost didn't want it to end. But all good things must.

The man walked to the far wall. He pushed his thumb into a keypad, and a metal fence rode along a track to the other side, sealing me off from the rest of the basement and eliminating any chance to get my hands on the tools.

Who the hell are these people?

The man left, slamming the door behind him and locking it. I stood up and walked to the fence. Grooves in the ceiling and floor secured the top and bottom in place. I wrapped my hands around the cool steel bars and tried to rattle them, but the barrier's magnificent structural integrity wouldn't allow it to budge. It was ingenious, really.

Fuckers.

That eliminated some suspects, at least. Some of the people I'd pissed off couldn't find their way out of a one-way hallway, let alone design something as complex as this basement prison. Unfortunately, it pushed the O'Rileys to the top of the list of suspects. They were excellent machinists. It had to be the Irish, but the masked man wasn't their don, Seamus, who preferred to be called James. *Could it be one of his sons?* Who the hell knew? I had a feeling I'd find out soon enough.

The worst part was that the man had left my revolver on the desk, just out of reach behind the fence. I loved that gun, and it physically hurt to see it lying there when I couldn't reach out and grab it.

I walked back to the wall and slid down it. My thoughts went to Gia. Would she understand I hadn't disappeared by choice? She had to know I wouldn't abandon her, even though I'd threatened her, told her to leave and find someone else if she wouldn't marry me. I wouldn't have let her, of course, because she was mine. She was too fucking important to let go. Even though I almost had. I thought things would be easier if we were apart. There'd be fewer complications if we could stay away from each other, but there was no way we would. We were addicted to the pleasure we gave one another. Gia let me fuck with her mind in the ways I loved, and I fucked her mind the way she craved.

We were perfect. A little toxic, but that never hurt anyone.

Except Silvio. Bullseye. Jameson.

I'd spent my whole life hurting people, and Gia was the one person I didn't want to hurt. Not like that, at least.

Chapter Twenty-Six

Gia

"I'm telling you, Marco, something is wrong!" I stepped in his path, blocking him from leaving the kitchen.

His dark eyes narrowed on me. "Goddamn it, girl. He does this. You two fight, and he runs off, as he has a tendency to do."

Enzo would leave for a little while to cool off, sure, but he *always* came back. And if he was talking about when Enzo went upstate, did he forget I was there, too? He wouldn't have gone without *me*.

"Will you just listen to me, Marco? It has to be the goddamn O'Rileys. They were the ones who shot at us!"

"How do you know?"

I swallowed. "Well, I don't know for sure, but I just . . . it has to be them."

"Enzo has plenty of enemies," Marco snapped as he pushed past me.

"How are you so cavalier about this? He's your brother!" I called as he walked away.

He didn't respond, and he seemed like he couldn't care less. It was maddening. If Enzo wasn't home by the time it got dark, I would talk to my father. He wouldn't care what happened to Enzo, but he cared about *me*, and maybe that would help.

Time ticked by, slow and dreadful. My mind raced. Was Enzo still alive? Was I chasing his ghost?

I dug through Enzo's drawers, trying to find anything that might give me a clue. I most wanted to find the address to the Irish pricks. It wouldn't be in with his deodorant and socks. I vaguely remembered the location of Jameson's shop upstate. I'd remember if it was in front of my face, but not the way to get there. I caught a glimpse of something that made me look twice—a black cellphone, flat against the wall of the drawer. I picked it up, half expecting it to be a secret phone. It was worse. It was Bullseye's fucking phone, the one I told him to throw in the river. I knew it was his because there was a big crack in the screen from Bullseye landing on it after Enzo shot him. A bullseye decal branded the back, and their family business logo sat in the corner. Yeah, it was his damn phone.

I pocketed the phone. Atheist whined before dropping his head to my lap. "I know, boy, I miss him, too. I'll find him." I would try to find him. No, I *would* find him. I just wasn't sure if he'd be dead or alive. I patted Atheist's silky head before getting up and putting on my jacket.

I PULLED up to my father's home. My home, though it felt less like it lately. I waved away guards as I pulled my car into the garage. My throat seemed to close up, as if warning me against this, but what choice did I have? If Enzo's piece of shit brother didn't care to help him, how did I expect my father to? He'd be aiding our relationship, which was something he didn't believe in. This was the solution to my father's problem, yet there I was, asking him to let go of animosity and years of rivalry to help me find Enzo. He'd happily let the problem sort itself out, even if it broke my heart.

A guard stopped me at the door leading into the house from the garage by putting the barrel of his rifle in my path. I gripped it and pushed it away from me. "Fuck off," I snarled. He knew who I was. He knew I was still part of this family, even if I was fucking the enemy.

With purpose-filled steps, I walked down the long hallway and grabbed the doorknob, inhaling a deep breath before opening the door. I knew my father would be there because he did his best business once darkness fell and the house was quiet.

I spotted his salt-and-pepper hair creeping over the back of his chair. The door slammed behind me, forcing his attention my way. His face was equal parts happiness and disappointment. I was certain he never thought he'd see me fall for a rival in his lifetime. He probably hoped he'd be long dead before a travesty of that magnitude occurred.

"Daddy," I said as I walked toward him.

His face softened with every step, as if he recognized me a little more the closer I got to him. It was a draw I knew he couldn't overlook. I leaned into him and breathed in his scent. He hesitated before wrapping his arms around me.

"You wouldn't come to me unless something was wrong," he said as he lifted my chin to look into my eyes.

"It's Enzo—" I began.

My father's posture tensed at the name. "What'd he do to you?"

"No, no, he didn't do anything to me." I took a deep breath. "He's missing, Daddy."

"And?" His features tightened, becoming smug.

"I think the Irish have him. His brother's a piece of shit, and—"

"Giovanna!" He stopped the words spilling from my lips with the harsh snap of my name. "Stop!" He put distance between us by standing and taking a few steps back.

"No, I need your help. I can't find him myself. I mean, I will, but I'd rather not."

His lips tightened. The fatherly bond was tightening its grip. He wouldn't want his only daughter to go against the Irish by herself. I was pushing him into a corner to force his hand.

"He's not my problem, Gia."

I turned to leave, but poison brewed beneath my tongue. I turned back to him, spitting venom. "He killed the man who put the bounty on your head. So, you're welcome."

My father's eyebrows drew together, his forehead wrinkling. "Who? Who was it?"

"Fucking Moretti."

"Ugo?" He took a faltering step toward me, as if tripped by disbelief.

"Don't look so surprised. You should have known it was him. Enzo just did what you wouldn't."

I took off for the door. My mind swirled with ways I could get Enzo back without the help of anyone else, but everything seemed like it'd end with my demise. But I had to try.

"Wait!" he called out. I shook the smile off my face before I turned to face him. "He really killed Ugo?"

"Tortured him, actually."

"Damn it." My father groaned as he rubbed the back of his neck. "Tell me about the Irish," he said with a sigh as he sat down.

<hr>

Enzo

THE SEARING hot pain of another fist ripped beneath my rib cage and weakened my legs. I kept on my feet, though not by choice. A man on either side held me up. The one to the left wore a rabbit mask, and the man on the right wore the white, smiling face of Guy Fawkes. The leader of their little group donned a Halloween mask with lit X's over the eyes and a bright, shit-eating grin across his mouth. A black hood covered his head and concealed every possible identifying feature. I could only see his hands and the shadow of his neck.

I spit blood to the floor, and a glob of it dripped from my chin as I panted through the pain. I could take punches. I fought for fun for a good portion of my life. I was never all that good about controlling my anger, especially once I got out of Silvio's grasp. Everyone became an enemy, and I fought enemies. Because of that, my pain tolerance was much higher than anything these fucks could dish out—as long as they didn't use tools.

"You know, you're supposed to ask questions and give me a chance to answer during these sessions." I spat more blood to the floor.

"There's nothing to ask. We know what you did."

"Then just kill me? Don't be such pussies about it." I stared at the grotesque red smile on his mask.

"Where's the fun in that, Mr. Viglione?"

"This is quite the party." A humorless laugh followed my words.

He grabbed a bat from the table, swinging it as he stepped toward me. He stopped in front of me and lifted the bat to his shoulder. "You are so fucking ballsy for someone in your particular predicament. Has your father taught you nothing? You need to learn to give up and be fucking quiet."

"Can't say Silvio was ever really a quiet man."

The man swung the bat, hitting me in the gut. I doubled over, choking on the air that rushed from my lungs. Blood-tinged drool fell down my chin, but the men at my sides kept a firm grip on my arms, so I couldn't even wipe it away. Yeah, I should have shut up, but it was better to go out while being a fucking asshole. I'd have more respect for someone who did that instead of crying and praying with their last breaths. I'd rather use mine to tell him where he could shove that fucking bat.

"Are you done, Viglione?" He stepped into me once more, lifting me by my hair. "You're lucky that Silvani girl was with her pops when we tried to get her. I would have *loved* the opportunity to show you what I would have done to her in front of you. Fuck, she's perfect. My men are waiting for her, though, so I haven't quite given up that dream yet." He laughed. "I'd have stripped her ass naked and forced you to watch as I fucked her. A girl like her would come from it. And then I'd put a bullet through her head because none of this would have happened if it wasn't for her."

Gia had nothing to do with anything. Not directly, at

least. If anything, she had tried to save Jameson by giving him her body. It was no one's fault but my own. I was certain they were the Irish. He'd given away too many things.

My dark, sadistic gaze met his eyes. Blood cascaded from my nose, staining my teeth when I spoke. I probably looked crazed. I was. He was lucky his goons held me back, because I'd have snapped his neck with my bare hands if I'd been given the opportunity.

He took a step back as the muscles in my body tensed and tightened. I leaped for him, dragging his men with me. I saw only that goddamn mask as I charged at him. His men reasserted their hold on me just before I could reach him.

"Fuck you," I said, spitting blood on his mask. It dripped over the red LED lights.

He raised the bat again. The sleeve of his sweater rose up his arm and revealed a bandage wrapped around his forearm. It was the last thing I saw before the bat arced in slow motion through the air, aimed for my head.

Chapter Twenty-Seven

Gia

A nervous excitement filled my gut. I always felt this way before my family and I went into battle. I double-checked my pistol and racked it. Ro's solemn eyes looked at me in the rearview mirror. My father's head rested against his fist. Neither wanted to risk their lives for Enzo, yet we were all risking our lives for him, even though he might have been dead already.

We drove to a steep hill and abandoned the car. Ro popped the trunk, and we loaded ourselves up. I tucked my pistol into the holster on my hip, picked up a rifle, and tugged the charging handle. I loaded a bullet into the chamber and put the sling around me, letting it hang at my side. Ro swung his rifle over his back, but my father opted for just his pistol. We'd cover him.

"You're sure he's with the Irish, Gia?" Ro asked.

I wasn't one hundred percent sure, but I was sure enough. "Yes."

"If he's not, we are making the biggest mistakes of our

lives. You know that, right? There'll be no coming back from it."

"I know, Ro," I snapped. If I was wrong, if my nagging gut wasn't correct, we'd end up dead for nothing.

The grass padded each step as we walked toward the big home in the valley between two lush hills. It made them sitting ducks. We wouldn't walk in like the movies portrayed, though. No, this was real life, and our lives were at stake. I lay in the grass, my family keeping watch as I rested the rifle in front of me and adjusted the cool metal against my cheek. I aimed the barrel toward the house and looked through the scope. The reticle followed the motion as I scanned the home. Two guards stood at the door. I had no clue how many could be on the outskirts of the premises or how many people might pour from the house at the sound of gunfire. Even though my weapon had a silencer, they'd know.

I wasn't a sniper, but I was fairly confident in my shot at this distance, and these men were posted, not moving as they guarded the front of the home. I placed the reticle center mass on the first man, just as my mother taught me growing up. The beat of my heart thumped in my ears, as if I were wearing headphones that drowned out everything but the sounds inside me. I inhaled, holding my breath as I curled my finger around the trigger. All it took was a small motion because the trigger was so light, and the weapon's power exploded in front of me. The gunshot rang out, breaking apart the silence of the night, and things moved unbelievably fast after the first shot. It's like a whirlwind, everything spinning around you while you feel stuck in time.

The man made a sound before collapsing and writhing on the ground. The other man looked in my direction, trying to draw the rifle hanging at his side. My heart hammered faster, and I sucked in air. That's why I wasn't a sniper. My panic could cost us our lives. I focused the reticle on the second man and finally got him in my sights before he could raise his rifle. I didn't have time to inhale. I had to pull the trigger.

My shot was too low. It brought him down but kept him in the fight. His blood-curdling scream cut through the night more than the gunshots.

"Fuck. Fuck." I got off the ground and we made a move before more people showed up. The second man crawled toward his rifle. I got to it before him, kicking it out of his reach as my father put a bullet in his head. The door opened and revealed another guard. He raised his rifle, and I fired into the doorway. Gunfire hailed from the balcony overlooking the hills. Ro raised his rifle and shot, and the sound of a body hitting the ground followed the ting of casings on the concrete. My heart slammed against my chest so hard, I thought it would rip through my skin.

I walked past the dead man. A river of red ran from his head. Judging by the look on his face, the first man I shot died soon after my bullet pierced his chest. He hadn't gotten that stunned expression they get when they realize they're dying alone, staring up at the night sky as their blood pools around them. I tried not to think of them as people once I killed them. I tried not to think about the family that would miss them.

Fuck. I was thinking about it.

Ro pushed me aside and opened the door with the barrel of his gun. I followed him, and my father kept watch behind us as we pushed through the house. An unarmed man popped out from behind a kitchen door, meeting the barrel of my rifle. His eyes widened as he threw his hands up. Words sped from his mouth in another language, and I narrowed my eyes on him before waving him off with my gun. He ran through the open door, screeching at the sight of the dead men.

"You're getting weak," Ro said.

"Fuck off."

"Leaving people alive is how you end up—"

"Ro, leave your sister alone. She made her decision," my father interrupted.

We turned the corner, coming face to face with a guard blocking a door in the long hall. He drew his weapon faster than we could react, and a searing heat tore through me. I didn't realize I'd been shot until I couldn't lift the rifle with my right arm. Blood poured down my white shirt and stained my skin. Fresh blood bubbled at the site of the wound. I let the rifle drop before leaning forward and cursing beneath my breath. Ro fired back, shooting the man dead. It was a rifle against a pistol, after all. My father pushed me against the wall and held his hand against the wound. I panted against the pain and kept my eyes locked on the silver chandeliers lining the hallway's ceiling.

"You'll be okay. You've had worse," my father whispered as blood spread around his hand. "We have to get you home, though." He tried to tug me away, but I refused to budge. I came too fucking close to stop now.

With a sharp inhale, I reached down to draw my pistol, but clenched my eyes closed as the movement made the pain course through my entire arm. I used my left hand instead. "Go, keep going," I told them. Neither made a move. "I said go!" I screamed the words, a desperate sound that made them push forward. All I could think about was saving Enzo. If there was something to guard behind that door, it had to be him.

Enzo

GUNSHOTS. Those were definitely gunshots. My head throbbed with a pain that radiated through my entire body. Blinking hurt. The two men dropped my arms, electing to draw their pistols instead. The man in front of me did the same. Whoever it was, they were walking into a trap.

The basement door opened, and boots rushed down the steps. Bullets sprayed from every direction. My first instinct was to drop and get cover, but I couldn't. I stared at that fucker in front of me. Smoke left his gun in slow motion as he shot toward the doorway. I leaped on him and ripped the stupid mask off his face. I knew who he was the moment I saw his arm, but seeing his face confirmed my suspicions.

"Now I know why my dog didn't like you," I said before punching him in the face. I ignored the pain in my stomach, ribs, and head. None of it mattered. I kept hitting him until his face became an unrecognizable mess beneath me, and I still couldn't stop. His words about Gia replayed in my mind.

The sound of gunshots rushed around me, and I remembered that I was in the middle of a fucking shootout. The two men hid within the shadows of machinery. They had the hometown advantage and knew every inch of this basement. I snapped my attention to the doorway, squinting my eyes at the pain from moving my neck. I couldn't believe what I saw. Was I dead? Had I already died?

Gia.

Not just Gia, but her fucking family. The people who despised me. I had to be dead, in some realm where I existed on memories and wishful thinking. My eyes followed a trail of blood running from Gia's shoulder. She was limp-wristing her pistol, shooting with her left hand as her right hung at her side.

"Goddamn it, Giovanna!" I screamed at her. I was so fucking glad to see her, but I couldn't handle losing her in a shootout with the Irish.

Sylvester tossed me the spare rifle in his hand. I caught it midair, despite the pain. The man beneath me gurgled on blood, and I pressed the barrel against his face as I shot. It obliterated him, spreading the blood across the floor and sending a spray onto the wall across the room. I climbed off him and raised the rifle as we pushed toward the back, where the other two men had run off. Shots erupted, muzzle blasts lighting up the darkness. I shot in that direction.

"Fuck," came the deep voice of Gia's father.

I spun around and saw the man with the rabbit mask. He'd flipped it upward, exposing his face to us all. His pistol barrel rested against Sylvester's head, and his body was partially hidden behind him. A human shield. I couldn't worry about that. He would die whether I accidentally hit him or if I missed the man entirely. I took a quick breath, stared down the barrel, and shot. Everything stopped but the motion of the bullet as it twisted down range. The man's head snapped back as his body jerked forward, and he fell to the ground with a heavy thud. The sound of a headshot.

Sylvester didn't hesitate as he aimed his pistol at me. Would he really kill me after all that? After saving his life twice?

He pulled the trigger.

That bullet traveled at an even slower speed than the last one, crawling across the air as I stared down the blast of light at the end of Sylvester's gun. The bullet whizzed by my head. I thought the old fuck had missed . . . until I heard the thud of another body behind me.

I turned my attention to Gia. She was pale and trembling from pain. I wound my hand through her hair and looked at her. Ain't no way I would let her die on me. No way. Not now. I turned to Sylvester, who still looked at me like he wanted the next bullet to go through me. Her brother looked even more pissed. Fair. I had no clue what my face looked like, but by the way Gia stared at me, I knew it was rough.

"Can I have your knife real quick?" I asked her brother, motioning to the large sheath on his hip.

He tugged it out and tossed it at me. I went to the headless Irishman and pulled his hand across the concrete before cutting off his thumb. I rushed to the keypad, put his thumb to it, and the door opened. There was no way I would leave my gun there, so I snatched it off the table, threw the rogue thumb toward its owner's body, and went back to Gia's side. I holstered my gun and brushed the sweat-soaked hair from Gia's face. She looked awful, even though she threw a comforting smile at me.

"We gotta go, Romeo and Juliet." Ro tugged at Gia's left arm.

Instinctively, I pushed his hand away. Her wound was still staining her perfect skin. She was so calm, though, which didn't surprise me one bit. Giovanna Silvani belonged in this life, and I was stupid for trying to keep her out of it.

Before we headed back up the stairs, I stopped for a quick glance at the man on the ground. The one who Atheist had attacked. I reached into his pocket and took his wallet, ripping his bloody ID from it. It was their second oldest son, Patrick. Fucking Irish pricks. Realization hit me harder than a bullet. My brother met with that man before all of this happened. I didn't want to believe it, but I had a sick feeling in my gut that he had something to do with it. Couldn't help but wonder if he shot my damn dog, too. Maybe that's why Atheist went all Cujo on him.

We met no opposition when we got to the main floor. We didn't kill their don, but I was fairly certain the three from the basement were his sons. The guards had been mere soldiers. I stepped over a body in front of the basement door. My eyes followed the blood trail, which was becoming gel instead of liquid—cold and sticky instead of warm and fluid.

"Wait," Gia said as we crossed the open doorway that led to a foyer. Jackets hung on hooks, and shoes dotted the room. Ro and I kept our guns raised and ready as Gia reached for her pocket. She winced as the pain seared through her arm.

I got behind her, reached into her right pocket, and pulled out a cellphone. Bullseye's phone. She holstered her pistol and snatched the phone from my hand. She stepped into the foyer and looked around, her eyes scanning the walls. There was a desk in the darkened corner, a set of keys sitting on top of it. She opened a drawer, turned the phone on, and slipped it inside. The welcome chime rang out, and she closed the drawer as if she'd never been there.

"There," she said with pride beaming off her. "The Irish killed Bullseye."

Fuck, that was smart. Why the hell had I never thought of it? And why was I so fucking turned on by her? It was *not* the time to look at her the way I was. Everything in me hurt, and she was injured. But those brains of hers? I shook away the thoughts racing through my mind. We had to go.

In the car, I sat in the back with Gia, despite her father's protest. I ripped off my shirt and held it to her wound. She didn't cry out in pain, but the sharp inhale showed me she was hurting.

"There's a home between here and the city. He's our veterinarian, and he can get her patched up."

"We have our own doctors, and they ain't for animals," Ro said.

"She's lost a lot of blood. Don't be stupid." I pushed my weight into her shoulder. Her blood soaked through my shirt and stained my hands. It was warm and wet and made me angrier with every drop. I was so fucking mad at her for putting herself at risk to save me, but I was also so goddamn in love with her for it.

I gave directions to the home of our vet. He was an animal doctor, but he was the best at mending those who couldn't—or shouldn't—go to the hospital. He also had the utmost discretion when it involved his human patients. No one would ever know we had gone to him, and we needed that certainty right now.

"Why'd you kill Ugo?" Sylvester turned and looked back at me.

"For her," I said as I brushed the wet hair from her cheek.

"Well, thank you, regardless," Sylvester said with a pinched smile.

"Don't do such stupid shit next time, old man," I said. I didn't want or need his gratitude. I didn't do it for him. I snaked my hand around the back of Gia's neck and drew her closer to me. "Why, Gia?" I whispered into her ear as I pulled her into me.

"Because you'd do it for me," she said as she dropped her head back.

"Can you go a little faster?" I said to Ro. She was fading. I knew she would the moment the adrenaline wore off, and I couldn't lose her. I refused to let her go.

We pulled into the driveway, and I got out of the car before Ro brought the car to a complete stop. I banged on the door. It felt like the night with Atheist, when I had knocked on the same door with someone else I loved bleeding in the backseat.

The doc opened the door, his white hair exploding in all directions from his head. He looked like he had been electrified. We'd probably woken him up.

"Holy shit, what happened to you?" he asked as his eyes moved down my body, hovering for much too long at my face.

"It doesn't matter. I need help."

"You gotta tell me more than that, Enzo," he said as he shrugged a robe on by the door, as if he kept it there just for these occasions. He wrapped it around himself and tied it off.

"Gunshot to the right shoulder." The words raced past my lips as he followed me out.

"Human or animal?" He tugged on gloves stashed in the robe pocket, probably also for these occasions.

"Human, and the most important one in the world to me." Desperation furrowed my brows and twisted my features.

The doctor opened the car door and looked at Gia. His lips pursed. She was no longer conscious. Sylvester awkwardly leaned between the front and back seat, trying to keep pressure on her shoulder. He looked at me with a hatred I deserved. I slipped past him and scooped her up in my arms.

"Wait here," I told Ro and Sylvester.

"I'm her father," Sylvester said, raising his tone sharply.

"Doc doesn't know you, so stay here. Let him work his magic," I told them before carrying her inside. The doc followed me, looking around frantically, as out of control as his hair.

"She needs a real hospital, Enzo," he said as he cleared his table with a brush of his arm, pushing everything to the floor. He tipped his head toward the table, and I laid her down. I kept my hand on her cheek as the doc checked her out. He lifted my shirt away from her wound, and the blood resumed its flow the moment it felt the air again. The doc put it back and lifted her to look at the back of her shoulder. "It's through and through, so you got that going for you," he said as he put her back down. She whimpered, and I rubbed her cheek.

The doc disappeared, coming back with sticks that looked like matches. "What's that?" I asked.

"Silver Nitrate. I need to cauterize so I can stitch her up." His voice lowered to a whisper as he talked to himself, working through his game plan. I didn't care what he did, I just needed him to fix her. "She's not going to survive without a blood transfusion," he said as he felt the pulse in her wrist.

"Can you do one here?"

The doc looked around frantically. He gathered supplies, laying them down on the table. "I can work with this. What's your blood type?" he asked me.

I raced through my memories of incidents that caused me to need blood of my own. "O negative."

"You sure? How sure are you?"

"Pretty sure."

"Hopefully you're right," he said, "because if you're wrong, you'll kill her."

Chapter Twenty-Eight

Gia

I slipped my dry tongue between my lips, but everything felt like cotton. The lids of my eyes were too heavy to open. I felt weightless and heavy at the same time, and I just wanted to go back to sleep. When I moved my shoulder, pain zapped my body like electricity. *Fuck, what happened?* At first, I thought I had died in the shootout, but I wouldn't expect to feel so fucking horrible in death. There was also a distinct lack of heat, which I would have felt if I'd died. Sent right to hell, no doubt. I groaned, which called the touch of a warm hand to my cheek.

"Gia," the voice said, but it seemed so far away, like it was miles above me.

I found the strength to open my eyes. Everything looked blurry, like I was looking through a pair of my daddy's glasses. I blinked heavily until my vision became my own again.

I was in my bedroom, and everything looked exactly how I'd left it. I turned my head and saw Enzo sitting beside me. He smiled at me, and I swore I saw gloss in his eyes as he dropped his gaze. His face was fucked. Bruises marked every inch of it, and one eye was still swollen and puffy. A bruise rose from beneath his blood-stained sleeveless shirt.

"Enzo," I whispered.

"I'm right here," he said as he pulled me into him, as gently as he could.

"What happened?"

"You got shot. I brought you to the doc who fixed up Atheist."

I sat up and rubbed my hand along the bandage. Everything came back to me—the Irish, the shootout, and rescuing Enzo. I remembered being in the backseat with him, but everything else was just . . . gone. "You brought me to a veterinarian?" I groaned as I tried to scoot back to rest against the headboard.

"A *really* good veterinarian," he said with a smirk.

"Why aren't we back at your place?" I looked around the room, wondering why he would stay within my father's home.

"Because if I went home, I'd have killed my brother, and I needed to talk to you about it first."

"Why me?" A cough slipped through my dry throat, and Enzo grabbed a glass of water waiting on the bedside table.

"Because you're better at this than I am," he said as he brushed back my hair.

The cool water filled my mouth and spilled from the corners of my lips, soothing everything it touched. I handed him the empty glass. "What the hell did they give me?"

He shrugged. "Some kind of animal tranquilizer."

"Perfect," I said with sarcasm.

"That was so fucking stupid, Gia." Enzo cupped my

cheek. "So fucking stupid. You could have died. If I die, that's one thing, but you can't die in a war that wasn't yours to fight."

I swallowed hard, my throat still feeling like sandpaper. "It may not be my war, but I'm your ally. I'll always go to battle for you."

"Fuck, I love you," he said as he tugged me into him. The sudden movement rocked my arm, and I winced.

I rubbed the bandage on my shoulder. "You know I love you. And my father knows it, too, or he wouldn't have helped us."

"Yeah, I still have doubts about him giving any type of blessing, Gia."

"He will." My words bubbled with confidence, but I really had no clue. I wanted to believe my father could let go of all that he hated about Enzo so I could be happy. I deserved to be happy. And it was the first time I ever felt that way.

Enzo leaned in to kiss me, but I pushed him away with my free hand. I didn't know how long I'd been out, but I knew I needed to brush my teeth. "Bathroom," I said as I climbed out of bed on legs that seemed disconnected from my body. Everything felt disconnected, like I was made of sand instead of blood and tissue. Animal tranquilizers would have been almost enjoyable if I hadn't had a hole in my goddamn shoulder.

I walked into my bathroom, closed the door, and looked at my reflection. My shirt had been ripped off, presumably to fix me up. Someone had put me in a dingy band tee with the name of the band too worn away to read. I splashed water on my face, flinching with every movement that used my right shoulder, which was most of them. I clumsily brushed my teeth with my left hand.

I returned to the bedroom on wobbly legs and sat on the bed. Before I could even get comfortable, Enzo's mouth was on mine. He kissed me hard. It felt like a thank you, even if he thought my actions had been incredibly stupid. He pulled away from me, wiped his chin, and covered his erection with his arm. He didn't need to cover it. I liked to see it, even if I couldn't do anything with it right then.

"What were you saying about your brother?" I asked.

"Oh, that fucker. I think he set it all up."

"Wha—how?"

"Remember the man Atheist mauled? The one who met with my brother?"

"Yes . . ."

"I saw the fucker's bandaged arm when his sleeve rose up, and when I ripped his mask off and saw it was him, I knew. Which means my brother set it up, or it's one giant coincidence."

I stared at him, gaping. "Do you think Marco would do that?" I recalled the way Marco reacted when I'd asked for help. He was so indifferent. Annoyed, even. He didn't act like a don's brother. "Fuck," I whispered. "He wouldn't help me find you, which is why I had to ask my father."

I had no doubt Marco was involved, but that was an ominous thought. That would mean Enzo would have to cast his brother out or kill him. I had a feeling I knew what he'd end up doing. Had I not been shot in the process, maybe he would have settled for exile, but not now. He would want retribution for my pain. Kicking him out of the family wouldn't be enough for him.

I COULD USE my arm after a few days. It still hurt, but not just from breathing. Enzo had come and gone, mostly to take care of Atheist and business. I was surprised my father even let him stay. A Viglione beneath his roof? Who'd have thought that would be allowed in this lifetime? I half expected Enzo to return, covered in blood after taking the opportunity to kill his brother when it presented itself. But I knew he'd want me there if he killed him.

The door leading into the courtyard opened. "I wish you'd lock the damn door," Enzo said as he came in.

I shrugged. I was pretty bad about that. "Did you see Marco?"

"Fucker can't even face me." He shook his head. "We need to get home. I've been neglecting my duties while taking care of you."

I sighed. "My father can take care of me, you know. I don't need you to disrupt your life for that."

"I ain't leaving you," Enzo said as he walked over and sat beside me. He kicked his shoes off and put his feet up. He leaned over and kissed my shoulder. "How are you feeling?"

"Better." I shook the bottle of pain pills and sighed. "It's so weird that my father is letting you stay here, in my bed."

"You're an adult."

"Yeah, but . . . you don't know my father." I smiled at the thought. My father was so protective of me, no matter what age I was.

"I've been so respectful of the sanctity of his home. Of his daughter," Enzo said with a growl that vibrated my body as he leaned into me. "Because you need to heal." He put his hand on my stomach and spread his fingers, dragging them downward. The touch electrified me, and my breath hitched as he palmed me over my shorts.

I put my hand over his, stopping him. "Don't get any ideas, Enzo. Not here."

"I want to make you come," he whispered before kissing me. "I ain't asking to fuck you, babygirl, but let me show you my appreciation."

"I don't need you to show me. Not here." I tried to speak firmly, but he climbed onto his knees and snuck between my legs, making the last words catch in my throat. They came out strained and unsure, and he took that as an invitation.

His hands climbed my body, and he tugged off my shorts. I stared at the bruises on his face as he spread my legs with a soft, tender touch that was very unlike Enzo. Even in a mask of purple, pink, and yellow, he was still so handsome.

"You'll have to be quiet," he said as he leaned down and rubbed his hand over my pussy.

I shivered, which made my arm twitch with an ounce of pain. I ignored it as his fingers pushed inside me.

"Fuck," he groaned, as if he wished his cock could be inside me instead. He leaned over and kissed me, thrusting in and out of me with greedy movements that matched the way he grinded the hard outline of his cock against my thigh. He groaned when I moaned, taking such pleasure in my sounds.

Enzo lay on his stomach. His arms hooked around my thighs as he eased me toward his mouth until his warm tongue was on me, making me jolt. Pain reminded me of my injury, and I tried to keep my shoulder still, which was more difficult with each slow, rhythmic movement of his tongue. He teased me until I wanted to buck my hips into his face and grind myself against his mouth. But if I moved my hips, it tensed my shoulders, causing pain all over again. I had to sit there, helpless and longing, as he licked me. I fought back a moan with a bite of my lip. If my father heard me, he'd kill us both. Enzo quickened the motion of his tongue, flicking the tip of it against my clit.

Pain and pleasure fought for control inside my body. The ache in my shoulder crawled beneath my skin and crept over my chest. The pleasure radiated from between my legs and rushed up to meet the hurt. I whimpered at the pain, but a moan followed close behind it. I expected him to stop as my body tensed and tightened.

"Come for me, Giovanna," he growled into my pussy. "Come against my mouth, but don't let your father hear you."

He buried his face into me and licked until pleasure overtook my body and pushed out the creeping pain. I gripped his hair with my left hand, ignoring the ache as I grinded my pussy against his mouth. I was so fucking close, but I still expected him to stop, and it made me tense with anticipation. I didn't want him to stop. I needed all the pain to count for something.

He swirled his tongue around my clit before tonguing me with a long, warm stroke that he'd repeat until I came. I put my left hand over my mouth and fought my chest's urge to rise off the bed as the pleasure became unbearable. I needed to come so fucking bad. I whimpered over my hand, needing to release some of the sound brewing beneath it.

He let me come. He rode out the waves of my orgasm with the heat of his tongue pressed against my clit. He rose to meet my mouth with his, my taste coating his lips.

"Good girl," he whispered as he placed his hand behind my neck and kissed me.

He was hard against the zipper of his pants, rubbing against the wet mess between my legs. He wanted to get off, too, but he wouldn't let me do anything more. He'd be inside me the moment he could, the very second I felt well enough for that. He'd ache with anticipation until I could give myself to him again, and I needed it as much as he did.

Soon, I promised him and myself. *Soon*.

Chapter Twenty-Nine

Enzo

I couldn't get enough of Gia. I soaked her in, enjoying the warmth of her body as she slept. I took in every inch of her with the tips of my fingers. I touched her as if it would be the last time I could, because recently, it almost had been. I had to push that thought away or the guilt would eat me alive, piece by piece, until I disappeared.

My face was healing and looked more normal by the day. My ribs still hurt like fuck, and I had to fight the pain with every breath. Nothing could be done for them. They just needed to heal. Like we all did.

What happened with the Irish could have—and should have—been much worse. They'd have killed me, but they would have kept me alive until they caught Gia and made her pay for my sins. They'd have made me watch them desecrate her, and that would have been a fate worse than death. But things didn't end like that, because Gia came in like a wildfire, willing to burn everything around us. She would rescue both of us or let us *all* get burned.

It had been a long time since I saw Gia in fight mode. Not since the subway, when she killed like a cold-hearted bitch. She had no fear. I never expected that from a woman, especially when she was so much younger back then. She looked just as hard when she burst through the door to the basement as she did in the shootout with my family.

I had tried so hard to keep her out of the lifestyle. I held her back, keeping her from the fray, the danger. What I saw that night showed me what Gia was capable of if I let go of my hold on her. By holding her back, I punished us all.

She even got my biggest enemy—her father—to join in on the big rescue. He probably wanted to leave me for dead. In fact, I was sure he would have. He didn't think I was good enough for his only daughter. I probably wasn't, but I loved her, and that had to be enough because I wouldn't accept any other answer when I asked for his blessing.

I stared at her while she slept, letting my eyes dart to her healing gunshot wound. If I had any chance of getting her father's blessing, it was gone the moment Gia got shot. No matter what, he'd see it as my fault, and it kind of was. But I never would have let Gia come in like the goddamn SWAT. If she died trying to save someone as destined for hell as I was, I wouldn't have forgiven myself. Losing myself was better than losing her. I'd have been dead; I wouldn't have known any different. But losing her while I still had breath in my body? Now that was hell. Not the eternal damnation, the demons, or the fire. It'd be returning home to an empty bed with an icy longing in my chest that made me pray for hell's fire to warm me.

My phone chimed. I reached over and checked it. It was a text from Bullseye's sister. I couldn't help but smirk as I read it.

It was the goddamn Irish.

Gia was a fucking genius. I hadn't even thought about the phone since I brought it back to the city, completely ignoring the nuclear problem that would eventually blow up in my face.

I squeezed out from under Gia's arm and got out of bed. I had a quick job to do, and I was sure Atheist was whining at the door by now. I tugged on my wrinkle-creased slacks and tucked the hem of my sleeveless t-shirt into them. I went over to Gia's side of the bed and kissed her forehead before leaving. The sun blinded me as I stepped outside, and I shielded my eyes as I walked to my car. A guard leaned against it.

"Get your ass off my damn car. So help me god, if there's one scratch, I'm going to cut your balls off and use your sack to buff it out."

The man pushed off my car. "Mr. Silvani wants to see you."

"Oh joy," I quipped as I leaned over and checked my car for scratches. "Looks like you can keep your nuts."

"Follow me," he said, annoyance furrowing his brow.

I followed him inside. I half expected Sylvester to yell at me for parking right out front. Wouldn't want to be seen harboring a Viglione, no doubt. God, what would people think if they found out he *saved* one? I was still amusing myself with these thoughts when the guard opened the office door and let me inside. When I saw what was behind the door, I sobered, tightening my expression. He was letting me into his office? His actual office? The most intimate place for a don. The library was where you conducted business, but the office was where you *created* it. He was allowing me access to the deepest part of his home.

I stopped at the doorway and peered into the room. A fancy wooden desk, the same color as the dark hardwoods it sat on, stood near a far wall. Sylvester's perfectly coiffed salt-and-pepper hair peeked above the back of a dark desk chair. A football game played on the big screen TV, and it had his full attention.

I cleared my throat, and he swiveled his chair to face me. I couldn't read his blank expression.

"Thank you," he said to the guard before waving him off. He turned his attention back to me. "Do you want a drink?" Sylvester walked to the glass fridge beneath the bay window. Frost licked at the glass and turned into smoke as he opened the door and rifled through bottles.

"It's noon on a Tuesday, sir," I said. It felt wrong to drink with him, and not because it was a Tuesday afternoon.

"Nonsense," Sylvester said, grabbing a bottle of bourbon and two glasses. He set them on the table and poured the rich, dark liquid. The glasses fogged from the chilled liquor. He handed a glass to me before sitting in his chair again. He took a long pull of his drink and placed it on a coaster.

I took a sip. Once it hit my lips, I fought the urge to chug it, thinking the alcohol might help ease the uncomfortable silence. He'd called me into his office, so he needed to speak first. He was testing me, trying to gauge my intentions.

"Mr. Viglione," he finally said. His voice was cool and nauseatingly calm, and that made me more uncomfortable. He should have yelled at me for drawing his daughter into a battle that wasn't hers. "Is it true? About Ugo?"

I patted the pocket of my slacks, feeling for my phone. I pulled it out, brought up a picture of Ugo, and slid the phone toward him. He raised his glasses and looked at the image of Ugo—tied up and bloody, but alive.

"Scroll over one," I said.

His mouth gaped as he saw the next picture. It was Ugo, very much dead and no longer a threat to Sylvester.

"Why?" he asked before lowering his glasses and returning my phone.

"For Gia. She won't marry me without your blessing," I said.

Sylvester shook his head before picking up his glass and taking another long sip. I expected his no. A big fucking N-O. I figured he might even pull that pistol on me to really hammer the point home. I would *never* marry his daughter.

"I don't want you marrying my daughter," Sylvester said. "I *really* don't want my daughter marrying you. She deserves the stars and the moon, not the small world you'd give her."

I knew it. I knew he would say no. "Her world is only small because I can't let her into more of it. I can't bring a Silvani into that part of my world. But I can bring a Viglione. I could give her the whole goddamn galaxy if she takes my name."

"How does that work for us? As families? Bringing the rival into your bed doesn't make them your ally in business. We all know that."

"Gia has never been my enemy, and I've never been yours. Shit, I shot my father to save *you*. I betrayed my family for *you*. For her." I shook my head. I actually called that sack of shit my father. "The hate for your family died with Silvio."

Sylvester rubbed his chin. "I'm going to be honest with you. I don't like this one fucking bit. I hate it, actually." He raised the tone of his voice as he stood. "I want Gia to marry someone I respect."

"Yeah, yeah, I know." I started to stand, ready to leave with the denial I expected.

"I respect you, Enzo."

I stopped dead in my tracks. Silvio had never said he respected me. In fact, he often told me how much he didn't. Hearing those words coming out of Sylvester's mouth made me feel a tinge of something that made my ribs ache.

"I give you my blessing."

I couldn't believe it. I wondered if I was dreaming, still asleep with my arm around Gia, longing for something I could never have. I dug my fingers into the palm of my hand to make sure I was awake. I was. I took a deep breath. I didn't want to act like a fool in front of him, even though excitement coursed through me. It felt like I had just secured the biggest deal of my life, and actually, I think I had.

I stood and reached my hand out to him, a symbol of truce. After he shook my hand, I turned to walk away, taking several steps before his voice interrupted my exit.

"Before you go," he said, "the Irish didn't kill Bullseye, did they?"

I tightened my lips. When my gaze fell, he knew. He had to know. He now had the secret he could dangle over me for the rest of my life. The secret that I killed Jameson over, which caused all the fuckery that followed. The secret that could get my ass put six feet under.

Sylvester picked up his glass, took a sip, and raised it toward me. He tipped his head with a smile. I had no choice but to trust him, but I hated giving that power to anyone. And now, the entire Silvani family had it.

I left his office. Part of me wanted to go tell Gia about her father's blessing. I fought that urge because I wanted even more to tell her while inside her. In the throes of her orgasm, I'd tell her she would be my goddamn wife. That she was mine.

Chapter Thirty

Gia

I parked my car in front of Enzo's house because I couldn't figure out how to get into the goddamn garage. The code he gave me didn't work, or I got the numbers mixed up, which was entirely possible. I had such brain fog since the shootout. I blamed the animal tranquilizer. Enzo had left before me and told me to carry my pistol on my hip when I came, which was suspicious. I dragged my fingers across the cool metal. A tinge of pain made me hope I didn't have a reason to draw and shoot, but I would if I had to. I hardly noticed the ache in my arm any longer. For an animal doctor, he'd patched me up real well. As the fibrous tissue replaced the once perfect skin on my shoulder, I knew I'd carry that memory with me forever, etched into my flesh.

When I walked into Enzo's home, everything was still. He'd been staying with me on and off, trying to avoid his brother. I racked my brain for some reason why Marco had met with the man who abducted Enzo, but I had nothing.

To my knowledge, they had no business with the Irish before. Atheist released a low whine as I closed the door behind me.

"Where's your dad?" I asked as I rubbed his head. "He told me he'd be here."

The sound of my heels on the marble floor carried through the space, so I took them off and walked barefoot instead, listening for any sound of life. The thick, heavy air ignited the sixth sense I inherited from growing up beneath a don. I felt the seismic waves of violence before I heard the shouts from behind the big wooden doors.

I quickened my steps and tried the door the moment I reached it. It was locked. *For fuck's sake.* I knocked, and the sound roared down the hall. Instead of an answer, something crashed inside. *Fuck it,* I thought as I tugged a bobby pin from my hair. I kneeled and tried to remember how to pick locks. I learned how when my father got me a lock-picking kit for my tenth birthday. Not the most age-appropriate gift, but if it worked, it worked. I bent the bobby pin and got to work on the lock. Once it clicked open, I abandoned my shoes by the door and walked inside.

Sammy was tied up in a computer chair against the wall. "Enzo, stop!" he called out. The tips of his fingers dripped blood onto his lap.

My eyes grew wider, and my mouth gaped at the sight. Enzo had Marco pinned beneath him. Marco wasn't even conscious any longer, yet Enzo continued hitting his blood-soaked face. Hitting a man who was too close to death to fight back created a hollow, disturbing sound. I put my finger to my mouth as I walked by Sammy. He groaned but stopped yelling out.

"Enzo!" I called out.

But he was gone, somewhere else entirely, somewhere

that was only a shade of red. I reached for his shoulder, and he flung himself back, knocking into me. I fell back against the desk.

"Sammy—" he snapped as he turned around with bloody fists. He blinked at me, as if he was being pulled back from that place full of anger. When he realized it was me, he sobered. "Gia," he said over the heavy rise and fall of his chest. He shook out his hand as he stepped toward me.

I didn't step back. I wasn't afraid of him, even when he wasn't being himself. I knew there was a part of Enzo that made him the perfect Viglione.

Violent.

Malicious.

A goddamn maniac like his father.

That part had always existed inside him, simmering beneath the surface.

"What have you done, Enzo?"

"He's lost his fuckin' mind!" Sammy yelled.

Enzo and I snapped our attention to him. I stepped in front of Enzo, stopping him from attacking his little brother. I glared at Sammy, trying to tell him to shut the fuck up with my eyes.

"Fucking came face to face with this prick," Enzo screamed as he wiped his chin with a bloody fist.

"What the hell are you doing to Sammy?"

"I had to know if he knew, so I used an Exacto blade beneath his fingernails." His eyes took on a dark, sadistic gleam.

"You tortured your own brother?" I looked at the sadness and anger all over Sammy's face.

Sammy's forehead creased. "I didn't know a damn thing!" he yelled before dropping his head back with a frustrated groan.

Enzo drew his revolver from his hip and walked back to Marco. When he raised his gun, aiming it at the ground, I put myself between them.

"Think about what you're doing, Enzo," I said. I needed him to think rationally for two fucking minutes. "How do you even know it was him?"

"Fucker admitted it. And he told me that the Irish prick shot Atheist. So get out of the way, Gia," he commanded. "There's no other way this can end for him. So move."

I shook my head.

"Suit yourself." He shot between my spread legs, putting a bullet into Marco's head and sending a spray of blood against my calves.

Sammy screamed.

I screamed.

Enzo was silent.

Thick crimson spread around Marco's head and crept around my bare feet. I hopped from one foot to the other, trying to get away from the blood, leaving red footprints in my wake. My ears were still ringing as I backed away from him.

Enzo stepped closer to Sammy, whose eyes were wide with panic. "Where does your allegiance lie, little brother?"

"I . . . I . . ."

I held my breath, because if he said, *"I don't know,"* he would be next.

"With you," he finally said.

Enzo's revolver hung at his side, twisting in his anxious grasp. I stared at Enzo. At the hard set in his jaw. At his dark and angry eyes. He reminded me of the Enzo I met so many years ago at the docks.

His hand went to my throat, the barrel of his gun grazing my cheek. I smelled the gunpowder. He leaned into me and backed me into the desk's cold wood. He squeezed my throat before dropping his hand from my neck to the hem of my skirt, where he clutched with a frustrated exhale.

"I want to fuck you, and I don't care if he watches," he gestured toward Sammy with the barrel of his gun. His words didn't surprise me like they surprised Sammy. Enzo didn't care who saw us together. He liked the power and possession of people seeing us. Or the risk of it, at least. I was his to show off, and he loved when people knew exactly who I belonged to.

Him.

"Leave her alone, Enzo," Sammy said, and my breath hitched as I mentally cursed him for saying anything. He didn't need to come to my defense. It's what Enzo had always done. Fucked out his frustration, and he was over-flowing with it. Sammy's words stopped his hand from creeping up my thigh. His eyes widened with something I'd never seen.

"Fuck," Enzo snapped. "What the hell am I doing?" He turned around and cut the ties that held Sammy to the chair, but Sammy looked too stunned to get up. He looked as if he was afraid to leave me with Enzo, but I was certain I could handle him, even in all his Viglione glory.

"Go!" I shouted. "Just go."

Sammy scrambled to his feet and took off, cradling his hands.

Enzo leaned over the desk, his jaw pulsing. "I almost fucked you in front of Sammy," he snarled, "but it would have made me like Silvio." He recoiled from his own words as if he'd never meant for them to tumble from his mouth. As if he'd spilled secrets he never intended to share with anyone. Not even me.

"Enzo . . ."

"No, no," he clutched his head, smearing blood on his cheek. "Don't ask me about it." He was in a frenzy from sharing a secret he'd intended to take to his grave. Saying it out loud made it all real. I knew that. I'd lived that myself. Admitting it made the pain tangible, and none of us wanted to feel that. But sometimes we had to. He needed to let it out because *that* had clearly been building up for a very long time.

His admission had sent him to some terrifying place in his mind. Probably where all that guilt and hatred lived. The place where Silvio was still able to hurt him.

He wasn't sane, so I kept my eyes on the gun twisting in his hand.

He lifted his revolver to gesture at me. My breath caught, but I brought my gaze up to his eyes and kept them there.

"You don't have to be ashamed of anything that happened to you," I said. I took a step forward and he took one back. I just wanted to get my hand on his gun, because Enzo, as I knew him, was gone. What was in front of me now was someone trying to confront their innermost demons.

Enzo

MY MIND WENT to a moment in my past. Silvio had a woman beside him, his pants unbuckled, his spent cock out. I wrapped my hands around a beer as I scooted to the furthest end of the couch. I had watched them. Him inside her. My fingers had gripped the bottle. Music played overhead, and blinding lights illuminated the stages. The bass rattled my chest.

"Come on, boy. If you're going to be a Viglione, you need to be a man."

I shook my head and raked my nails against the glass bottle. I tried to say no. I tried. But he made me fuck her after he had. And it felt good. That was the worst part.

"I tried to say no," I said out loud. I felt the revolver's weight in my hand. "He got hard," I said in a strained voice. I twisted the gun at my side. I was stuck in a memory that broke me, a secret no one knew the extent of besides my dog.

The familiar sound of nails clicking on wood met my ears, and there was a tongue against my hand. A harsh whine pushed inside my mind and drowned out everything else. The stage disappeared. Silvio vanished. I dropped the gun, and it thundered as it hit the ground. I fell to my knees and buried my face in Atheist's neck, crying as I pulled him closer. His soft coat warmed my hands, which had begun to feel like ice. I looked up, blinking away any signs of weakness, trying to hide the fear that made my body tremble against my will. Gia was kneeling in front of me, her hand on my revolver, dragging it away from me.

I expected to find fear on her face. I thought she'd look at me like I was fucked up. Because I was. Instead, she nudged Atheist out of the way and wrapped her arms around me. She held me in a grasp that I melted into. I looked behind her and saw Marco. All the blood. I sighed. It was going to happen anyway, but it shouldn't have happened like that. When I saw him, when he looked in my eyes with disappointment on his face, I fucking lost it. And Sammy. Fuck. He was . . . I just had to know he wasn't involved. I couldn't lose both of them. But I probably already had. I sighed and sat back on my heels, pulling myself out of her grasp.

"Well, fuck," I said as I dropped my head back. Energy drained from every muscle inside me, as if it was sucked out of me the moment the adrenaline left my body.

What happened, what my galloping heart was still trying to recover from, was too fucking much. The pure anger that ripped through me transformed into my need to release my frustration through Gia, like it always did, but taking her in front of my brother would have made me too close to Silvio and his sick, twisted showmanship. Admitting that to her? *That's* what tossed me into the deepest depths of my mind and made me panic. It trapped me inside a quicksand field of memories. I never wanted her to know what happened to me. I needed to be strong and instead, was only weak. Her knowing made me feel lighter and heavier at the same time. Lighter because I *finally* told someone about what Silvio did to me. And heavier because I was certain she'd never look at me the same way again.

I struggled to look at Gia. She wouldn't want to marry that Enzo, the Enzo that was capable of the blood hanging in the air. I had shed more Viglione blood. Betrayed another one of my flesh and put the fear of God in the other. Actually, it wasn't the fear of God. It was the fear of me. And it would spill onto Gia one day.

I stood up, dragged her to her feet, and pulled her against my chest. I just needed to feel her because when everything was wrong, she always felt right.

Chapter Thirty-One

Gia

Enzo had fallen asleep on the couch after he showered and washed off the memories of last night. He'd shown weakness and strength. I knew something happened to him as a child. That was why he celebrated the death of his father instead of mourning him.

I took a shower after him, drowning my own memory of yesterday. Wet strands of hair circled my head, dampening the pillow. I turned over and sighed. I couldn't sleep. I got out of bed and tugged down the hem of his sleeveless t-shirt I was wearing. The frayed fabric grazed my thigh. I went to the drawer, grabbed the cigarettes, and pulled one out.

Stagnant night air greeted me as I stepped onto the patio. I lit the end of my cigarette and puffed on it. My damp hair made the sleeveless shirt stick to my skin. Enzo came up beside me and reached for a cigarette. I gave him mine and lit myself a new one. He put it between his lips and leaned over the railing, balancing on his elbows as he wiped his hands through his hair.

"I'm sorry, Gia."

"You need to apologize to Sammy, not me," I said as I inhaled.

"I will." The smoke swirled around us. "I don't know what happened to me in there." He turned and leaned his back against the metal railing.

"You bottled shit up, that's what happened."

"Ain't no one wants to hear about a don who was a puppet for his father." He sighed.

"Did he . . . do anything to you?"

Enzo dropped his gaze. "Nah. Just had me do things in front of him. Or he did things in front of me." He admitted his secret, his words growing lighter at the end, as if the weight was being lifted off his shoulders.

"I wouldn't have judged you."

He let his blue eyes meet mine. "I know," he said with a pinched smile.

It was true. I didn't judge him for what happened to him. It explained why he was the way he was, but I didn't judge him for that. If I was going to be with Enzo, I had to accept that his father still coursed through his veins, even once the man was long gone.

I put my head on his shoulder, and he pulled me into his warm, bare chest. I sighed against him, inhaling his scent. So much happened so fast. At least he had people to take care of Marco. I didn't think he could handle seeing him again.

Enzo leaned down and lifted my chin with a soft, tender touch that was so unlike him. His lips hovered in front of mine. His hand dragged back, tugging loose hair with it. I kissed him and tried to forget all the bad shit that had happened. His fingers grazed my shoulder, reminding me of what I'd do for him. The hurt in his eyes reminded me of the things he'd do for me.

He kissed me back, spreading my lips as his tongue ran along my teeth. His throat vibrated with a growl.

"It's not the same patio," he said as he turned me around, put my hands on the railing, and got behind me.

His hands moved over my body, slow and patient. They stopped at my chest, and he squeezed the flesh beneath the thin fabric of his shirt. They dropped lower, trailing along my hips until he reached my thighs. He raised the shirt's hem until it met my waist. He lowered his sweatpants, letting the heat of his cock rest against my bare skin as he kissed my shoulder where the bullet had exited.

"Do you remember what you said to me as I spread your thighs that night?" he whispered as he opened my legs with his knee.

I shook my head. I really didn't remember. It was so long ago, and I wasn't totally sober.

"One time. You'll get me just one time like this. Make it count. That's what you said as you pressed your ass into me just like this. I tried to move on from you. You were a goddamn Silvani. We shouldn't have been doing what we were doing. Fucking our enemies," he growled as he pressed his hips into me. "But I couldn't get enough of you. I couldn't let it happen only once. Even as you stand here, with my cock against your ass, you're still just a Silvani."

I groaned and dropped my head back. The banter between us wasn't so different from back then. I remembered telling Enzo not too long ago that we could stop being enemies for one night. One time. But once I had him again, I couldn't let it be just one time, either.

"Please," I begged. I needed him right then, more than ever.

"What do you want, Giovanna?" he whispered in my ear as he put his cock between my legs and rubbed his fingers against my clit.

I moaned into the night air. "I want you to fuck me."

Enzo turned me around, lifted me, and put me on the railing. The metal bit into my ass, and I squealed as I teetered on it. I grabbed his shoulders, lacing my hands behind his neck.

"Do you trust me?" he asked as he grabbed my hips and leaned down so all I could grab was the mess of his dark hair.

"Not really, no," I said as I tried to gather my bearings. He had a firm grasp on me, and I knew he wouldn't let me fall, but if I looked down at all, I got off balance.

He couldn't force my legs apart, not while he was holding on to me. I inhaled and opened them myself, deciding to trust him.

Enzo licked between my legs, hungrier than he'd ever been. His fingers gripped me, digging into my flesh. I moaned as I grabbed more of his hair. My thighs wanted to clench around him because I felt more unbalanced the more his tongue moved on me.

I began to tense.

"I'm not going to let you come, babygirl," he growled against my clit. "Not until I'm done with you."

I dropped my head back, my hair playing in the wind as I looked up at an ocean of stars. I gripped his hair and pulled him deeper into me to anchor myself so I didn't fall. I knew he wouldn't let me fall, but fuck if I didn't feel all that fear in that moment as if he would. Tension raked my body and fear electrified every inch of me, but the fear turned into more and I started to tense in a whole different way—a way Enzo recognized all too well.

He stood up and pulled me from the edge in a literal and metaphorical way. I leaned back against the railing with heavy breaths, partially from the pleasure and excitement, but also because I was glad to have my feet back on the ground. He lifted my thigh with his hand and pushed inside me as if he couldn't wait a moment longer. I dropped my head again, much like I had on the railing, but my eyes were still closed. He made me see stars behind my eyelids. That's how fucking good he was. His thrusts were slow but strong, and the pleasure took off from where he'd left me. The pulse of his hips against mine put me right back on that edge. His cock stretched me and brought me close again. I was that driven to come. My thighs trembled and my stomach tightened. The pleasure chased me, but I fought it. If he felt my orgasm coming, he'd stop. He'd take it away and leave me a mess of desperate frustration.

Like clockwork, he let my body tense and throb until I was on the edge of my orgasm before he pulled out of me, and I felt a longing for him the moment he did. He brushed my cheek with the back of his hand.

"I told you, I won't let you come until I'm done with you. Suck my cock while you step back from that edge."

I dropped to my knees, and he kept his eyes on me as my knees hit the concrete. His cock glistened with my wetness.

"Taste yourself, babygirl."

I took him into my mouth without hesitation. I loved his cock. Every curve of it. Even the drops of salty come on the tip of it, showing me just how excited I made him. I tasted the sweetness of my pussy and licked up his cock, slow and sensual. He uttered an impatient growl, but I wanted to tease him like he'd teased me. I swirled my tongue around him, and his thighs tensed.

His hand fisted my hair and tugged, and I moaned at the pleasurable pain from his hold on me. Enzo put his other hand behind my head and thrust his cock into the back of my throat. I fought the gag as he held me there. I struggled for air but enjoyed every moment of his unearthly groan as he twitched in my mouth.

"Such a good girl," he whispered as he pulled me off his dick. A string of drool hung from my chin. "You look so damn beautiful with your lips all red from my cock. With the drool on your chin." He wiped at my skin. "Cheeks all flushed." His hand grazed my cheek. "As much as I want to keep you down there, keep your mouth on me, I need what's between your legs."

⌖

Enzo

GIA WAS ABSOLUTELY stunning on her knees. The locks of her soft black hair wrapped around my fist. Her dark eyes overflowed with desire. She wanted more. As stunning as she was, I needed her pussy. I wanted to be inside her again. I didn't even need her to suck me off, I just needed her to do something with her mouth until she stopped being so close to the edge. I'd let Gia come, just not yet.

I wanted her driven mad first. Angry and frustrated.

I dragged her back to her feet and kissed her. Her cheeks were still flushed, and it crept down her chest as my tongue pried into her mouth. I couldn't get enough of the way she tasted or how she smelled. I loved those intoxicating whimpers of pleasure and the delicious sound of her frustration.

I let my hand hover over her cheek. She still wanted me, even after seeing me for who I am, the parts of me I couldn't always hide. She'd learned things about me that I'd never told another human soul. She saw me at my weakest moment.

And she still wanted me.

There was so much I needed to take care of regarding my brother's death, but instead, I had Gia's body against me. Yeah, my priorities were fucked, but I had no intention of pushing Gia away. Not when the swells of her breasts strained against my sleeveless shirt. Not when she bit her lip like that.

I dragged her inside and closed the door behind us. I shooed Atheist off the bed, and he protested with a groan before sliding to the floor. I kissed her again before laying her on her back. Her chest begged to spill from the sleeveless shirt, so I reached out and ripped the thin material. I grabbed her breast and teased her nipple with my tongue. She arched her back beneath me. I slipped my sweatpants further down my thighs, taking them off.

I let my cock rest against her slick, warm pussy. I twitched as I thrust my hips forward, rubbing her clit with the length of my dick. I wanted to push inside her so goddamn bad, but I wanted to tease her more. I kissed her again as I thrust, slow and shallow, gliding against her. She whimpered, filling my mouth with her frustration. She reached down to put me inside her, and I pinned her wrists above her head. Her annoyed glare would become anger if I kept rubbing my warmth against her perfect fucking pussy.

Did she not realize how hard it was for *me?* How much blood left my body to fill my dick, aching with the need for her? It was maddening to feel my curves graze over her swollen clit. It felt so *fucking* good. I couldn't stop thinking about pulling back a little farther, enough to let the next thrust be inside her. That was what she wanted, too, as she raised her chest to meet mine.

"What do you want, Giovanna?"

She rocked her hips beneath me instead of answering.

I shook her wrists in my grasp. "No, use your words."

"I need you, Enzo. Stop the games. Just give me what I need." Her words snapped at the end. She was getting mad, and it made me throb.

I captured her wrists in one hand, letting the other rove down her body, landing on her hip. "You know, if you didn't act so needy, I wouldn't have any fun playing these games." I squeezed her hip. "If you didn't need me so badly, you'd have me by now. I'd have finished you off out there on the balcony. But I like the way you come when you're angry, how you feel around me when I finally let you."

"Fuck you. You're an asshole," she snarled, and it made me smile. She wasn't kidding. Her face twisted, and she tried to pull out of my grasp.

I let go of her wrists and fisted her hair, lifting her head and craning her neck until her lips were close to mine. I growled as I kissed her. I gave in, drawing back, sliding my tip along her skin, and pushing into her with a thrust of my hips. She was so warm, so damn wet. Everything I couldn't stop thinking about. She gripped the sheets beneath us.

"Is that what you wanted, babygirl?" I drew back and pushed my hips into hers.

She screamed out before nodding her head. I gave her exactly what she wanted as I fucked her how she liked—the selfish way that made her come the hardest on my dick, as if she was only there to make me come, like I was giving her a gift by fucking her. I was addicted to how it made her clench around me.

I lowered my head, putting my lips against her ear. "You're a fucking Silvani," I said with the disgust she craved. She squeezed me, just as I wanted, choking my dick in a wave of pleasure inside her.

I rolled over, pulled her onto my lap, and kissed her before drawing her chest to my mouth so I could get my hands and mouth on her perfect tits. They filled my hands as I drew her nipple into my mouth. I put it between my teeth and bit, increasing the pressure until she screamed out for me to stop. Then I gave it just a little more before releasing her.

Gia reached down and gripped me, putting me inside her. She lowered herself onto me, and I groaned as she took me deeper until I felt the very end of her. She couldn't take any more of me. Not on her own. I fisted her hair, drew her chest to mine, and thrust upward, burying myself fully inside her. She bit her lip to keep from crying out. Her excitement dripped down the length of my dick as she raised herself before coming back down on me.

So damn wet.

I let go of her hair and put my hands on her ass instead. My fingers dug into her flesh as I squeezed. She rocked her pelvis on me until her motions grew ragged. Her body tightened and tensed. She was so goddamn close. And so was I. The ache in my balls crept up my lower back, but I'd fight it until she came hard on my dick.

I wrapped my arms around her waist and drew her into me as she grinded against my pelvis with guarded moans, expecting me to stop her. Her breath hitched, waiting for me to snatch her orgasm from her. She'd had enough, and I couldn't hold out any longer myself.

"By the way . . ." I slowed her movement, flashing my eyes up at her. "You're going to be my fucking wife."

"Wh-what?" she panted. She stopped and stared at me, wide eyed.

"I got your father's blessing," I told her with a smirk. I basked in her motionlessness for a few moments. My cock twitched inside her.

"H-how?" She looked dumbstruck, as if she was hearing something that couldn't be possible. I once thought the same thing.

"Don't worry about it, just worry about coming on my dick," I whispered as I drew her in for a kiss. I thrust, letting her ride out her shock while still dangling her over the edge.

"I'm going to be your wife?" she asked as she grinded against me.

"You're going to be a Viglione, Giovanna," I said before kissing her. I fisted her hair and pulled her lips off mine. "But if you don't come now, you won't come at all."

My words made her spasm around me. She sat up, her long hair falling over her shoulders, and she rode me. I kept my hands on her hips, guiding her motions. She looked incredible, and I was going to come whether she did or not.

I groaned as I tried to fight it off, but it was happening. "I'm coming," I said as I dug my hands into her hips.

"Me too," she said through a moan as she came with me, hard as fuck. She clenched around me, drawing everything from my cock. I tugged her into me and wrapped my arms around her as a gravelly moan left my lips.

It was earth shattering.

The strength of her orgasm made mine stronger. It created a sensation I'd never felt in my life. Nothing even came close to the pleasure that coursed through me from her body.

She collapsed against my chest. Her skin was sticky with sweat. I reached over, opened a drawer, and felt around for what I wanted to give her. I pulled it out and closed my fingers around the metal. Giovanna looked up at me as I brushed her wet hair from her face. My hand reached for hers as I stared back at her.

"What are you doing?" she asked, her breaths still laced with her orgasm.

"Making it official," I said with a smirk as I slipped the large princess-cut diamond ring onto her finger. The delicate filigree around the band glistened with more diamonds. Her eyes snapped from me to the ring.

"You just had a ring lying around like that? Who else were you trying to marry, Enzo?" she asked with the smallest hint of serious accusation.

"Don't talk your shit while my cock is still inside you, Gia. It's my mother's ring. And you're the only person I would give it to."

Her eyes rose back to mine, a smile stretching across her features. Her finger grazed the ring. She deserved even more than that, but my mother would have wanted this. Maybe not the whole marrying a Silvani part, but she would want the woman I would kill and die for to wear her ring.

We were both spent. The world disappeared around us as I listened to her heavy breaths. There was no looming death, no business, nothing but her and me. Nothing but an impending wedding—a forced truce as we merged our families.

Epilogue

Gia

Our officiant was not happy. He wasn't the cheery man who married so many of our family and closest friends. Instead, his lips were tight and his brow furrowed. He brushed a hand through his white hair before he began.

My eyes scanned the rows of seats. My family was on one side, and the dwindling Vigliones sat on the other. His brother was well dressed and had a hint of a smile on his face. Sammy forgave Enzo. After everyone had the chance to cool down, it was as if nothing had ever happened. But Sammy was easier to befriend without Marco around. We weren't there yet, but we were getting there. I recognized his business partners and his friends; they'd taken the seats vacated by the missing members of his family. My gaze landed on my father. He was less angry looking than the officiant, who was bitter about the union. He had been on our books for my entire life. He married my parents, for Christ's sake.

There was such a mix of expressions in the crowd, and I

expected it. I knew our families wouldn't merge without flaws. I knew I wouldn't be accepted right away as a Viglione. I needed to be okay with it. I could worm into their hearts if they gave me the chance. Until then, I'd deal with the harsh stares and hushed words when I was around.

"Yada, yada, husband and wife. You can kiss," the officiant said.

I smirked at him. I appreciated him for tying a knot that shouldn't have been tied. Not in this lifetime. Even if he couldn't hold back the distaste, he'd married us.

I looked at Enzo, in his rich black suit, freshly pressed, with a purple dress shirt underneath. A dark tie draped over his chest. He looked so goddamn handsome. My breasts, raised by the corset of my wedding dress, drew his gaze. He kept his hands in front of his lap, and I knew why. The moment we left the church and got home, he'd tear that dress off me.

He stepped into me and wrapped me up in his arms. He kissed me hard and passionately in a possessive show of ownership that I welcomed. The officiant groaned beside us —an audible sound of disgust that made us smirk.

We pulled away from our kiss, and I turned back to the crowd. My father was standing, his lip quivering, fighting a smile on his face. He motioned me toward him. I let go of Enzo's hand and ran to my father, letting him embrace me.

"You look so beautiful, Giovanna." His eyes were glassy. "Enzo looks alright, too," he said as Enzo came up beside me.

They shook hands, but my father drew him in for a hug. He whispered something in Enzo's ear, and it made him smile. Probably something about killing him if he hurt me. Which was fair.

I walked around, greeting as many people as I could

before the gloss in my eyes blinded me. Enzo came up beside me and leaned into my ear.

"Bathroom," he commanded.

I shook hands with Kenny, and he hugged me. "You look beautiful, Gia. Welcome to the family," he said as he pulled away from me.

I carried my heels as I walked to the back of the church. I popped into the bathroom. Enzo was leaning against the wall, unable to wipe the smile off his face. "My fucking wife," he said with a growl as he circled me.

"Not here," I said as he picked me up and put me on the countertop. "We're in a goddamn church, Enzo!"

He flashed his eyes up at me, a devilish grin on his face that lit the fires of hell inside me. "When have you ever cared about sins?"

He was right. I'd fuck him in front of God himself. I'd lie down with him in front of the devil.

The door opened and Sammy came in. His eyes scanned my bare thighs where my dress had ridden up.

"For fuck's sake, Enzo, it's a church!" Sammy snapped. Enzo looked at him through the mirror, an intense gaze on his face. He reached beneath his jacket, tugged out his revolver, and aimed it at the door.

"I'm going to fuck my wife, Sammy. Right here. Right now. In this goddamn church." His eyes darkened. "So get the hell out before I tack on another sin."

Sammy shook his head and left, the door slamming behind him. Enzo tucked his gun away. "Should we lock it?" I asked as Enzo's hand dropped between my legs.

"No, fuck 'em. If they come in, they won't only see me closer to sin, but fucking inside it."

Enzo pulled me off the counter and bent me over the marbled top. His zipper lowered as he bundled my dress at my waist. He moved my panties aside and pushed inside me. His hand reached for my throat, and he lifted my chest off the counter. The squeeze made my head swim.

"You aren't a Silvani anymore, Giovanna. You're my wife. A Viglione," he growled as he thrust in long, hard strokes. "You're mine. You've been mine since I was first inside you. Even when I fought it and put us through hell to get us here, I was yours. You had me wrapped around your crazy little finger. Without you, having an empire means nothing. Without you, I'm nothing."

"I love you, Enzo," I panted as he squeezed my throat.

Enzo leaned over and kissed my bare shoulder. "I've only ever loved you. But as I get close to filling you for the first time as my wife, I want you to remember that I will give you everything you want in this world, except every orgasm you chase. I will hold some of them out of reach because I love your desperation. I love the way you move when you want me to make you come so badly that it hurts."

"Please don't hold it this time," I begged. "It's our wedding day."

He grazed my clit for several strokes. "I'm going to come now, but I'll make it up to you tonight. I want to lay you down on *our* bed and fuck you in *our* home. I'm going to devour you like you're *my* last supper. I won't stop until you're a come-soaked mess and I'll have to cleanse you of our sins with my tongue."

Enzo pulled out of me, turned me around, and lifted me back onto the counter. His blue eyes locked on mine as he stroked the warm heat of his cock against my slit. I dropped my head back and moaned as he came on me and moved my panties back into place. With a dark smirk, he pulled me off the counter and gave me a quick rub between my legs. "You know what I like. You're going to go through the rest of this evening wearing my come."

"Enzo, no!" I said, though I knew it was futile by the look on his face—the sadistic look that made me melt.

"Be glad I'm letting you keep your panties on this time," he said as he tugged down my dress and smoothed it out. The warmth of his come saturated the fabric between my legs.

We're going to get spanked in hell by the devil for this.

Everything about us was sinful, which was fitting for two people destined for hell. And I wouldn't have had it any other way.

More to come...

Closer to Sin ends The Sin Duet, but not the world contained in these pages! Join my Patreon to take part in polls and offer reader input for the future of this world! Patreon.com/LaurenBielAuthor. Join in on discussions in Lauren Biel's Traumances on Facebook.

Connect with Lauren

Check out LaurenBiel.com to sign up for the newsletter and get VIP (free and first) access to Lauren's spicy novellas and other bonus content!

Join the group on Facebook to connect with other fans and to discuss the books with the author. Visit http://www.face book.com/groups/laurenbieltraumances for more!

Lauren is now on Patreon! Get access to even more content and sneak peeks at upcoming novels. Check it out at www. patreon.com/LaurenBielAuthor to learn more!

Acknowledgments

Thank you to my husband for continuing to stick by me through this journey even though I'm a temperamental mess.

I'm sending out another thank you to my unicorn readers, who continue to support me! Christina, Kolleen, Terri, Danielle G., and Ash. You guys are the BEST Beta and/or ARC readers and friends! Love you!

A special shout out to my patrons:

Christian, Kimberly B., Jay, Jessica, Ariel, and Ash V.!

About the Author

Lauren Biel is an author with several titles in the works. When she's not working, she's writing. When she's not writing, she's spending time with her husband, her friends, or her pets. You might also find her on a horseback trail ride or sitting beside a waterfall in Upstate New York. When reading her work, expect the unexpected.

To be the first to know about her upcoming titles, please visit www.LaurenBiel.com.

9 798986 869780